INSIDE THESE WALLS

IRIS BAXTER

© 2023 by Iris Baxter

All rights reserved. No portion of this book may be reproduced mechanically, electronically, or by any other means, including photocopying, without permission of the publisher or author except in the case of brief quotations embodied in critical articles and reviews. It is illegal to copy this book, post it to a website, or distribute it by any other means without permission from the publisher or author.

"The true discomfort of being watched isn't the eyes fixed upon you, but the disconcerting awareness that someone holds the key to your vulnerability without your consent."

    — Unknown

Contents

Chapter 1 7

Chapter 2 15

Chapter 3 25

Chapter 4 31

Chapter 5 37

Chapter 6 47

Chapter 7 51

Chapter 8 55

Chapter 9 67

Chapter 10 73

Chapter 11 79

Chapter 12 85

Chapter 13 93

Chapter 14 97

Chapter 15 107

Chapter 16 117

Chapter 17 127

Chapter 18 135

Chapter 19 143

Chapter 20 147

Chapter 21 155

Chapter 22 163

Chapter 23 173

Chapter 24 177
Chapter 25 185
Chapter 26 191
Chapter 27... 197
More Books by the author 203

For everyone who is against the lack of privacy that plagues the modern era.

Chapter 1

I must be dreaming. There's no way a place like this is so cheap.

Each corner the landlord Mr. Sunderland shows me into, I'm in awe. Not only is the location of the apartment amazing—only ten minutes from my workplace—but it's pretty spacious and luxuriously-equipped.

When I first entered the apartment five minutes ago, I was sure I had the wrong place. That's even what I told Mr. Sunderland. The ad I saw said the rent was only $800 a month and required one month's worth of deposit.

A place like the one I was standing inside went well over $2000 in a bad location. In this one, it could go for as much as double.

"No, you're in the right place, Andrea," Mr. Sunderland says. "The reason why I didn't put any pictures up on the ad is because it attracts all sorts of... locusts, if you get what I mean."

He's a handsome man in his late thirties. On top of being slightly nervous about looking for an apartment, I'm also nervous around him because he's good-looking. I keep chuckling like a schoolgirl at everything he says, and I hope he's not noticing it.

It's been a while since I looked at another man that way. But ever since I broke up with my ex...

"Yeah, I understand," I tell him with a nod. "This place is amazing."

I avert my gaze to the apartment. It's so big I feel like I could do gymnastics in it. Not that I'm able to, but still. It gives me so much space. I do consider how time-consuming cleaning is going to be, but I don't care. Right now, I desperately need a place of my own. Something I can be comfortable in, if not call home. Something that's going to make the stress of a long day vanish as soon as I get cocooned in the safety of the place.

Mr. Sunderland says, "Well, I do try to keep up with the times and renovate the place every now and again. Over here, you can turn on these fancy lights." He flips a switch, and purple overhead lights bathe the kitchen counter. "You also have an AC in both the living room and the bedroom. There used to be one only in the living room, but sleeping with just that one during summer can be difficult because the heat doesn't reach the bedroom as well."

My eyes drift to a blank wall between the entrance and the kitchen. The rest of the apartment is decorated with this or that, but this part of the apartment looks too empty. There's nothing there. Not even a framed picture.

It's just a wall.

"How come you left that part so empty?" I point.

"Oh," Mr. Sunderland says. "The wall there is different quality than the rest of the apartment and will need renovating in the future. See?"

He knocks on the wall, and it produces a hollow thud.

"It's not a hazard, though, is it?" I ask.

"Absolutely not, Andrea. I provide only the highest quality. This is only one part that I still haven't fully upgraded to the quality it deserves," Mr. Sunderland says.

"I see." I nod.

My mind is too hung up on how amazing this place is to worry about some useless, hollow wall, or any other flaws it might have.

The apartment consists of a big living room, a bedroom, and a fancy bathroom. Once my initial excitement wanes, a thought occurs to me, one that has been looming above my head from the moment I stepped inside but remained suppressed because of my excitement. Now, it resurfaces once more and hits me like a splash of cold water to the face while I'm asleep.

Something's wrong with this place. Something that's not visible at first glance, but it's gotta be here. Why else would it be so cheap? I'm searching for faults of the apartment to justify the cheap rent. There's gotta be something wrong with it, right? There's no way in hell someone would rent out such a nice place for such a low price, no matter how selfless they are.

"Say, there aren't any rodents or insects in this place, are there?" I ask.

I'm searching for something Mr. Sunderland might have conveniently left out that would reveal why the price is so low. At the same time, I'm hoping all the answers are negative.

Mr. Sunderland chortles. "Of course not. I personally can't stand bugs, especially roaches, so I make sure to do a full inspection every now and again to make sure everything's clean."

I hate roaches, too, I want to say in excitement, but I stop myself from doing so.

I don't think I've ever met a man who worries about infestations. Whenever I panicked over a bug getting into the apartment, Ryan would roll his eyes and make me feel like I was making a big deal. He would squash it or throw it out, sure, but his reaction made me not want to tell him about it in the first place. Eventually, I started to get rid of the stray bugs on my own.

Now, it would become a habit if I moved to this place.

"Any problematic neighbors?" I ask.

Mr. Sunderland shakes his head. "Maybe a few nosy ones, but it's a perfectly safe building and neighborhood, I assure you, Andrea."

What could it be, then? Maybe the utilities are too high? They will naturally be more expensive in a spacious apartment like this one, but how much should I expect to pay?

"So, that's all the rooms, Andrea. I live just down the hall in apartment 407," Mr. Sunderland says. "So, if you need any repairs or find any faults with the place, you can knock on my door, and I'll come fix it right away, Andrea."

He often says my name. I'm usually annoyed when people do it, but for Mr. Sunderland, it seems to be natural.

I'm bothered by the last thing he said, though.

So that's the whole trick. The landlord lives right here. Does he give his tenants trouble? Does he represent himself as this polite man only to become a living nightmare the moment they sign the lease? Does he stop by unannounced?

I've heard many landlord-related horror stories from other people. Like, my friend Becca said she once had an old landlady lock her out of the apartment she was leasing because she didn't like the fact that Becca brought her boyfriend home.

Then my college buddy James said that his landlord would be at his door at 5 a.m. on the first of every month with a checklist to make sure everything was still in place—including the toilet, as if he would tear it out of the ground and steal it.

Then my cousin Miranda said she once rented a place for a few days where the landlord invited her to a threesome with his wife.

Mr. Sunderland seems nice, though. It's refreshing. It gives off an aura of reliability. I don't know if something hides beneath that, but if dealing with a pesky landlord from time to time is all it takes to snatch up such a place for so cheap, I'll gladly bite the bullet.

Besides, beggars can't be choosers.

I need a place as soon as possible since I've just broken up with my boyfriend and moved out of his apartment. All my friends had told me not to move in with him, but I didn't listen to them.

Hindsight is 20/20, right?

I've spent the past month living with my friend Becca and her boyfriend Jacob. While I enjoy spending time with Becca, I can tell there are moments when I'm intruding. The two of them live in a small apartment, and with me being there, they don't always have the privacy that people in a relationship need.

That's why I'm in such a hurry to find a new place. That, and the fact that I feel vulnerable and weak without my own place to stay. I'm grateful eternally to Becca, but it's time to move out. Doesn't matter that she keeps reassuring me I'm no bother.

I really should have thought about the possibility of being in this situation while dating Ryan, but I had thought that he and I would last forever. I never thought I'd even need to consider the reality of being in the situation that I'm in right now.

Love does crazy things to us. It blinds us, robs us of our rational thinking, and then leaves us naked and scarred.

That's okay. I've learned the hard way. I'll be more careful next time.

I sound very indifferent about it, I know, but trust me, that's not the case. I'm still very hurt that Ryan and I ended our two-year relationship, but I'm keeping my mind occupied because it keeps the dark thoughts at bay.

I'll have time to think and cry. Right now is not that time.

Right now I need to find a new place to live in.

I'm strangely excited about it. As difficult as a clean slate can be, it's also full of promise.

"So, what do you think, Andrea?" Mr. Sunderland asks.

He's flashing me a polite smile. As handsome as he is, he looks even better when he's smiling.

"I love the place," I say. I can't think of any other questions, so I decide to be direct. "I just don't understand why it's so cheap. I mean, don't get me wrong, but is there something wrong with it? Did someone die in it or something?"

Mr. Sunderland throws his head back and guffaws. "You're funny. No, nothing like that. I can assure you, the place is as good as it gets." He grows serious and says, "I understand your paranoia, Andrea. I'd be careful, too, if I found a place like this so cheap. The reason why I don't charge more is because, well, you can see what's happening to the real-estate market right now, yeah?"

I nod. The prices to lease and buy real estate have gone sky-high recently. And they keep growing.

Let's just say I can forget about ever owning a place of my own if it continues this way. I'm in the same boat as millions of other Americans trying to save up money for a house.

Between battling inflation and low wages, buying a house has become fantasy. It's all about surviving until the end of the month now.

"Well, I've had a few tenants who have struggled with money immensely," Mr. Sunderland says. "I was blessed enough to get an apartment from my parents and to be able to buy this place before this real-estate madness took over. I thought I'd help someone by making it slightly easier for them, you know? Give back to the world somehow."

"That's very kind of you, Mr. Sunderland," I say.

"Please, call me Lee," he says.

"Lee. Okay." I nod.

I like that name. I like how it sounds on my tongue.

"Believe me, if I could, I'd rent this place out for free, but I got bills to pay, too," he says with a chuckle.

"I understand. It's really noble of you to bring the price down like that. I appreciate it."

He waves a hand. "Money is the root of all evil. I used to work twelve and fourteen-hour shifts, chasing overtime to afford luxurious things I didn't even need. I don't care about that anymore. I'm happy with what I have. I don't earn too much but enough to get by. That's more than I can ask for and definitely more than a lot of others can say."

I crack a smile at that. His words sound so genuine. I can't be sure if he's full of crap or not, but in that moment, I believe him, and I like him all the more because of it.

"Regarding the tenants on this floor, you won't have any problems with them. It's all people around our age. I think I might even be the oldest one on our floor." He lets out a peal of laughter. "Everybody respects the rules here. So, no loud music late at night and whatnot. There are some annoying residents on other floors, especially some I personally can't stand, but you won't have to see them much save for the occasional elevator ride."

I nod. I appreciate he's open about what the residents of the building are like and not sugarcoating the place to be this perfect utopia where everyone is sitting around the campfire, holding hands, and dancing.

"So…" He puts his hands on his hips. "Whaddya say? Interested in getting this place?"

To be frank, I *love* the place, but I really want to think about it before I jump into the decision. In a last-ditch effort, I look around the place as if I'll find something faulty in these last few seconds. The truth is, I've already made up my mind.

I am going to move in here, one way or another. Now I'm just searching for a reason to solidify that decision.

I turn to Lee and I say, "Where do I sign?"

Chapter 2

Becca and Jacob offer to help me move my stuff to my new apartment, but I tell them it's not necessary. I don't have too many things to move anyway. Just a few boxes.

I left most of my things at Ryan's place because I was too distressed to go through everything and pack it properly. When we broke up, the only thing that was on my mind was getting the hell out of there as fast as possible.

Sometimes, I replay it all in my head. I spent every waking moment of the weeks leading up to the break-up dreading my own emotions. I would look at Ryan and realize that the only thing I felt for him anymore was an echo of the past. It didn't matter how much I tried to convince myself otherwise.

I would fear being left alone, because that meant overthinking, but being in Ryan's presence was even worse, because I would force myself to feel something—anything—just to dispel the nothingness that lingered in my mind.

It didn't help that he had been oblivious the entire time. He would kiss me, tell me he loved me, ask if I wanted to grab lunch or dinner or watch a movie. He would go about his day like everything was okay. For all he knew, it was.

Still, him being so ignorant to my distance made me wonder whether he really knew me. It helped solidify my theory that things were coming to an end. I spent days coming up with the courage to tell him it was over, but every time I looked at him and opened my mouth to speak, the words refused to come out.

It happened one night when he returned late from the bar. Him drinking with his friends had become just another in the line of things I disliked about him. I had been tolerating it for a long time, and now I suddenly couldn't stand anything this man did. As if my brain was preparing me for the break-up, to somehow make it easier on me.

It wasn't the drinking per se. It was the fact that we had so many different hobbies and interests. He's an extrovert, I'm an introvert. That is not a problem itself, but the fact that we seemed to be on different paths was.

All he wanted to do was earn enough money to get by and have fun on the weekends. I, on the other hand, want to have a lucrative job, to get a bank loan one day, to buy a place of my own, to settle down and have a family.

It was as if we had been on the same level when we met, but then we somehow drifted apart. I'd hate to say it, but I think I'm the one who grew and moved on while he stayed on the same level as when we met.

He sat down next to me, gave me a kiss—his breath smelled of beer—and said something about not having work tomorrow and not going out anywhere. I had asked him if he had gym, and he said he would skip it because he didn't feel like going.

That was the last straw for me. The words just flew out of me before I could even stop them. "I think we should break up."

There was silence for a long, long time. Ryan didn't understand where this was coming from. For all he knew, this had come out of the blue. Things between us had been fine, fine, fine.

Except they hadn't been. Problems were piling up under the rug so much that it had become a mountainous terrain too big for two people to clean up. It was both our faults. Mine for not talking to him enough, and his for dismissing what little I did tell him.

I'll never forget that night when I packed my things. Ryan had pretty much given up on talking to me by then, so he sat in silence, staring at his phone, ignoring me as I buzzed from one room to another. I'll never forget how invisible I felt that night, how Ryan's expression changed from a long-time relationship partner to that of a stranger.

I wanted him to stop me. To say something. Anything. To promise he would change, even if it meant he would be lying. I was so weak that I would have agreed to anything. Just one more chance. Maybe this time it would work.

Except it wouldn't, and just like that, a two-year long relationship was over.

People sometimes drift apart. Friends, family, lovers… That's a normal thing in life. It's something I keep telling myself whenever I miss Ryan. I know I don't miss *him*. I miss what we had in the past, and that's never coming back.

Now it's too late to go back and tell him I want to get my stuff. Besides, I have a feeling he might contact me about that sooner or later. He's going to try to use it as an excuse to get me to meet with him, but I won't fall for it. I won't see him, because I don't trust myself to stay strong enough to resist him.

"The moment you say yes to him is the moment you'll allow yourself to be drawn back into that relationship again," Becca had told me multiple times, and I agreed with her.

While staying with her and Jacob I managed to keep my thoughts occupied, which helped me immensely. It held the pain at bay… for the most part.

Either way, I don't care about Ryan right now because I'm too pissed about trying to fit all my boxes into the elevator so I can get to the fourth floor. Most of the stuff fits except the computer chair that I took from Ryan's apartment.

That chair has helped alleviate my back pain immensely on the days when I work from home, and I'll be damned if I leave it to Ryan. He wouldn't even use it, and it would only collect dust over there.

"Stupid thing," I say as I try to fit the chair in from multiple angles but to no avail.

Someone walks up behind me and looks at the elevator cluttered with boxes. It's a woman pushing a baby stroller. We share an awkward look with each other as her eyes expectantly flit from me to the elevator.

"Sorry," I say. "I'll try to unload these as fast as I can and send the elevator back down to you."

"It's okay. We'll take the stairs," the woman says and reaches into the stroller.

The baby inside lets out a small cry until her mother silences her with a soft cooing noise.

"My name's Andrea. I just moved here," I say.

"Uh-huh," the woman absent-mindedly says, but she doesn't introduce herself.

I guess she's too busy carrying the baby and moving the stroller to the side.

"What floor do you live on?" I ask.

"Ninth," she says.

"That's gonna be a lot of climbing. Give me five minutes to get these out, and I'll send the elevator back to you."

"Don't worry about it. Since you blocked the elevator, we'll take the stairs. I have to feed her soon anyway," she says with a smile that doesn't reflect in her eyes and cheeks; only her mouth.

I open my mouth to respond to the "you blocked the elevator" remark, but I don't know what to say. Do I apologize? Do I tell her I don't appreciate her passive-aggressive remark? Before I can think of a proper comeback, she's already turned away from me and has continued climbing the stairs.

Fine. Walk, then.

Maybe keeping quiet is the best way to go anyway. I do understand that she needs to feed her baby, but it's not my fault I didn't know she would need to use the elevator so soon.

Since the chair won't fit, I leave it outside, step inside the elevator among all the boxes, and press number four. A patina of sweat covers my forehead and armpits, and I'm out of breath. Standing in the elevator for the short time that it ascends gives me a moment to catch my breath—but only a moment.

As soon as the doors open, I drag the boxes out one by one. I don't take them to the apartment just yet. I first need to free up the elevator in case anyone else needs to use it.

Since you blocked the elevator, we'll take the stairs, the woman's voice clings to my thoughts. I hate that the sentence is probably going to haunt me for the rest of the day.

Once the boxes are out, I take the elevator back down. I hope no one steals my stuff during the few minutes that I'm gone.

When I return to the ground floor, I pick up the chair and start climbing the stairs. I barely make it to the second floor when I realize what an arduous task this is going to be.

I'm panting, sweat is breaking out on my forehead and temples so much that it's sliding down my face, and my arms are burning from carrying all the stuff upstairs.

Okay, I may have overestimated myself. Maybe Becca and Jacob's help would have come in handy here.

When I climb the next flight of stairs, I'm forced to put the chair down. Then it hits me—it's a chair. I sit on it and lean my back against the rest, exhaling a deep sigh. I close my eyes and imagine how beautiful it would be to take a nap right now.

I don't care if anyone sees me sitting in a chair in the middle of a stairwell. I don't care if they need to go around me. I just need a break.

No time for that. Work now, sleep later.

I'll get my things inside, and then I can order some food, take a shower, and nap. I can unpack my boxes later tonight or tomorrow, I don't even care.

I force myself to stand from the comfortable chair. The muscles in my legs scream in protest at that, but I don't listen to them. I groan as I grab the chair and lift it off the ground. Sitting for a moment was a mistake because it now feels as though the thing has anchors attached to it.

I lift it with a huff and prepare to climb the next set of stairs when I see a figure descending from the top. I step aside to let them pass so I can have more wiggle room, but then I recognize the figure.

"Hey, Andrea. How's the move going?" Lee asks.

"Oh, good, good. I'm almost done," I say, trying to hide how out of breath I am.

He stops in front of me, and I can tell he wants to chat, so I put the chair down to conserve my energy. I'm too aware of the sweat on my face and under my armpits. If Lee is noticing it, and he must be noticing it, he's not giving any indication of it.

"The chair didn't fit in the elevator, huh?" he asks. "Let me help you with that."

"Oh, no. It's okay. I can handle it," I say, but in my mind, I'm screaming *Yes, please do it for me.*

He's already picking up the chair despite what I said, and he turns to me to say, "It's no trouble at all. Let me at least help you with this."

He starts climbing the stairs, and I go after him. My arms feel like they're weightless now that they don't need to strain to carry anything heavy.

"Thank you, Lee," I say, following him.

"Don't mention it. You got anything else downstairs that needs carrying?"

"No. I sent all my other things to the fourth floor. I just need to get them inside the apartment."

"I'll help you do that."

I'm flattered he's offering to help me.

When we get to floor four, he puts the chair down and smiles. He didn't even break a sweat, and his breathing is only slightly faster. He's in good shape, it seems.

"There," he says. "Now, let's get those boxes in."

I unlock the apartment and open the door wide. The first thing I get inside is that chair. I haven't decided yet where I'm going to keep it. Probably the living room since that looks like the most comfortable place to work from during work-from-home days.

I won't have my own separate office here like I did back when I lived with Ryan, but it's all right. I'll make do with what I can.

"You planned on lugging all of this by yourself? Geez, Andrea. You're either incredibly strong or have no sense of how heavy this stuff is," Lee said.

"I'm just bad at calculating things. When I flew out to Alaska, I did so with one thin jacket and tennis shoes. And that was during winter time."

"Ouch. How come you don't have anyone helping you move?" Lee asks as he effortlessly brings the last of the boxes inside and puts it on the kitchen counter.

"My friend and her boyfriend offered to help, but I said no. I didn't want to bother them," I say. "But, lucky for me, you were here to help me. Thank you for that."

"Don't worry about it. Do you need help with anything else, or…?"

"No, I think that's all of it."

Lee puts his hands on his hips and looks around the apartment and the things we hauled inside. I can see what he's thinking even before he says it.

"That's not a lot of things, is it? Are you sure this is all of it?"

I don't want to talk about why I brought such a small number of things here, so I say, "Yeah. I didn't want to overburden myself like last time, so I brought only what I need."

"What about things of sentimental importance? Things that mean a lot to you because you have a memory tied to them?"

I left those with Ryan.

"Well, I'm sort of a minimalist," I lie.

Lee nods. I can't tell if he believes me. "You need to add your touch to the place where you live. I think this place would liven up a bit if you just decorated it with some of your personal things. Some stuff hanging on the walls, decorations on shelves and tables, hell, even a paint job if this color is not your cup of tea. It would go from being an apartment you're renting to home."

I give him a courteous smile. I haven't even moved in yet, so I don't really view this apartment as my home, but I appreciate that Lee is giving me the freedom to do whatever I like with it. "I'll be sure to do that, but I wouldn't want to overshadow the hard work you put into making this apartment look the way it does."

"No, by all means, go ahead. I want you to feel at home, Andrea. Because that's what it is."

I smile again and pretend to shuffle one of the boxes across the floor, just to break eye contact with him. I don't want him to see something in my eyes that I wouldn't like to reveal. Something about Lee tells me he can read me more than he's letting on.

"Well, I'll let you get unpacked and settled in then," he says a moment later and turns to leave.

"Thank you so much again for helping me. I feel bad for taking up your time with this," I say.

"It's fine, Andrea. I'm happy to help."

He's at the door when I say, "Lee?"

He spins to face me.

"I was gonna order some food," I say. "Let me repay the favor by treating you to a meal."

Lee looks like he's contemplating the offer.

"Oh, you must be tired. I wouldn't want to intrude," he says.

"You wouldn't be intruding. Come on. After everything you did for me, paying for a meal is the least I can do."

Lee considers that for a moment, then throws his hands up and says, "Okay. Sure."

Chapter 3

We opted for Chinese. You can never go wrong with Chinese food. We're sitting in the living room, eating at the coffee table while the boxes are messily strewn around us.

It's bittersweet to me.

There's something magical in moving into a new place on that first day and having that food break while your things are still packed. It's a promise of a new life. Of good things to come.

It reminds me too much of the day I moved in with Ryan. I had thought that the next time I moved, I would have been carrying Ryan's last name, and it would be moving into a house we bought together.

He and I talked a lot about getting a house in the countryside. Some place surrounded by tall trees, preferably in Oregon. I always wanted to live there. It's painful to think that'll never happen. It's even more painful to see all the unopened boxes in my new apartment and him not being here to share that moment with me.

The first week after the breakup was the hardest, but many of the things are only now starting to hit me. I had foolishly thought I was in the clear and that I wouldn't be sad about the breakup, but that's just another in the line of mistakes I've made.

Becca went out of her way to keep me occupied. When I felt like crawling into the earth the most, she forced me to get out of bed, take a shower, and dragged me outside. Spending time at the mall and buying expensive things I didn't need helped a lot, but all of it was just delaying the pain.

"So, what brings you here anyway?" Lee asks.

I'm glad he's here. I don't think I can stand the loneliness right now. Him eating with me and talking to me helps take my mind off the looming, dark thoughts that are just waiting to bite into my mind.

After careful consideration, I wonder whether there's need for me to tell Lee the truth. If I start talking about Ryan and the breakup, I probably won't be able to stop. These things usually work that way when they catch momentum.

I'm also afraid of crying in front of Lee. It would be really awkward for the both of us. He's been nothing but kind to me, and I should return the favor somehow.

But when I look at Lee, I can somehow sense him reading me again, and I know lying will be too obvious.

"Well, I lived with my boyfriend until recently, but then we broke up," I say before I can stop myself.

It feels both good and bad to say that. Voicing my problem makes me feel as if I've just vomited out something that has been making me sick for a long time. At the same time, I fear the questions that will follow up.

"Oh, no. I'm sorry to hear that," Lee says, but doesn't ask anything else. He's probably polite enough not to poke and prod, but I find myself *hoping* he'll ask me more, to give me an excuse to vent.

"Yeah. It was pretty tough. Still is. I mean, we only broke up a month ago," I say.

"How long were you together for?"

"Two years."

Lee nods.

"We had problems for a while toward the end," I continue. "I guess we held a lot of grudges."

"Against each other?" Lee asks.

"Yeah. Me against him for not accepting a job offer and generally being more ambitious, him at me for not being more supportive, and... Well, I guess we were too late to work something out." I realize I've said too much despite not wanting to go into details. Something about Lee makes me want to open up to him. And I can see how intently he's listening to me. I find that so attractive in a man.

Maybe I'm just looking for what Ryan wouldn't give me. I could talk to him about my day, and he'd nod and say, "Uh-huh," while being fully focused on a video game he was playing. After a while, I stopped opening up about the stuff that happened at work, and later, even the important things.

That was just one of the many factors that contributed to the downfall of our relationship. Anyway, looking for a culprit will do me no good. It's over, and getting answers won't fix anything. Looking backward would only cause more pain.

I can only look forward from here.

"Sorry," I say when I realize I've said too much to Lee, who is probably not interested in my life's drama. I move my gaze away from him in embarrassment.

"Don't apologize. Break-ups are tough," he says. "Especially when you've been with someone for so long."

"Yeah."

"I guess we kind of tend to lull ourselves into this sense of..." He squints at the ceiling, searching for the right word. "Normalcy, I guess? We think the person's going to be around forever, so when reality knocks on the door... well, it's not pleasant."

Now he's the one who looks like he's regretting saying too much. Lee sounds like he's speaking from experience. I feel compelled to ask him about it, but it would be inappropriate. If he feels like it, he's going to tell me about it.

Otherwise, I'm not going to push.

"Do you live alone in your place?" I ask after I deem enough time has passed for me to safely change the topic.

I'm not trying to ask if he's married or in a relationship. I mean, I'm okay with him telling me, but I'm not actively trying to find out.

"Yeah," Lee says. "I moved here a few years ago when my mother left the apartment to me. I had planned on buying my own place before that, but then I saw this place was up for sale. I had enough money for a down payment, so I took the plunge."

"How come you're not staying in this apartment and renting the one your mom gave you?"

"First of all, this apartment is too big for me."

"Too big?" My eyes grow wide.

He laughs. "Yeah. Too much cleaning to be done. The one I live in is a one-bedroom apartment. It's more than enough for a man like me, and I'm happy with that. I don't need anything more than that."

Does that mean he's single? Maybe he has a girlfriend he doesn't live with.

"What if you ever decide to get married or have a family?" I'm the one who's poking around now. I want to find out if he has a girlfriend at least.

Lee flashes me a vague smile. "I'll cross that bridge when I get to it. Right now, I'm happy with minimalism."

I like that he's humble and clearly doesn't care about material possessions.

"So, what are the other tenants like? You told me what the others are like on our floor, but you also said there are some you dislike?" I ask.

"Depends on what floor you visit. There's at least one obnoxious or weird person on every floor except ours."

"Really?"

"Yeah. On the first floor, for example, there's Ms. Willis, who complains whenever there's noise. Sometimes, people order food or use the elevator, and she knocks on doors to check if they know who it was. On the fifth floor, there's a writer who rarely leaves his apartment. I've never met him, and he's supposedly been living here for five years. There's a running joke here that, if you walk past his apartment when the building is really quiet, you can hear clacking of a typewriter's keyboards."

"It's like a ghost story." I chuckle.

"Right. On the ninth floor, you have the Turner family that thinks they're the most important in the building because they have a baby."

"I think I met them. A woman with long, black hair?"

"Yup. Her name's Samantha."

"She got angry at me for blocking the elevator with boxes."

Lee shook his head. "Typical of her. People don't like them because they argue with everyone about the smallest things, and they're always going to use their baby as an excuse. Don't walk in the hallways too loudly because the baby is sleeping. Don't flush the toilet at night because the noise travels, and the baby is sleeping."

"Good thing we're not on the same floor as them."

"You'll still suffer their presence because they're practically living in the elevator. That's another reason why people don't like them."

"What do you mean? They use it a lot?"

"Yeah. You've seen how slow the elevator is, right? Whenever I tried using it, it would either be on the ninth floor or all the way down on B1 when they go to use the garage. I got impatient and started using the stairs. Best thing I decided to do."

"Because of waiting?"

"That and extra cardio."

We chuckle at that. We finish eating our food and continue talking some more.

"By the way, I'd offer you a drink, but I don't have anything except water in here," I say. "I'd go out and buy beers or something, but I gotta take a shower and unpack the rest of the stuff."

It's a subtle way of saying *I would like to be alone now, please, and thank you.* Don't get me wrong, I'm enjoying Lee's company, but I haven't had proper alone time in over a month.

"Don't worry about it. I should get going anyway, too." Lee slaps his knees and stands. "Thanks for the food, Andrea."

"Thank you for the help, Lee."

"If you ever need anything related to the apartment or otherwise, you know where to find me."

"Thank you."

I see him out, wish him a nice day, and close the door. Now that the day's passing, I'm starting to feel the exhaustion of the move creeping into my body. I can't wait to crawl into bed. God, I hope the mattress is not too soft. My back always hurts in the morning from soft mattresses.

But first, a scalding bath. This apartment has a big bathtub, and I'm going to use the heck out of it. The warm water is going to help with my exhaustion. I'm suddenly giddy with excitement about that. It's always the small things that bring us joy.

With those thoughts, I go into the bathroom.

Chapter 4

Lee unlocks the apartment door and steps inside. He's feeling pretty content with the fact that he's spent time with Andrea. Now he just needs to play his cards right and something beautiful could be born out of it.

He could hardly take his eyes off of her the entire time. He knew he couldn't stare, so he sneaked glances at her when she wasn't looking.

He thought he could feel a spark between them. It was something tiny and barely noticeable, but it was there. Lee will make sure to nurture it until the spark becomes an ember, and the amber turns into a fire. He is already off to a good start with Andrea.

When he locks the door and enters the living room, he notices a face staring at him from the darkness. He realizes he's been smiling when his lips droop. Lee reaches for the light switch and flicks it on.

The room is bathed in a pale light, and Lee spends a moment staring at the old woman in the wheelchair. Only a few white strands of her hair remain on her scalp. Her cheeks are sunken, eyes bulging out of the deep sockets. The stare is that of a braindead person, but Lee knows well that an intelligence lurks behind those eyes.

"Hello, Mother," Lee says as he enters the kitchen and turns on the stove. "Sorry for being late."

"Where have you been?" the old woman asks him with a croaky voice.

Lee puts a pot with leftover food on the stove to heat it up. She's been preparing to attack him, probably for hours now. She's had nothing but time, and she's spent that time running dialogues in her head.

"That's none of your business," he says.

"You've been with the new tenant, haven't you?" his mother asks.

Lee's lips stiffen. He leans on the counter, hoping the old bat will stop pestering him. He can feel her milky eyes on the back of his head, though. He should know better than to think she's going to drop the conversation so easily.

"Answer me!" she says.

Lee turns around to face her. Her eyes are plastered to him and her lower lip is quivering.

"Yes," Lee says. "But there's no need to worry, Mother. I only helped her bring her boxes in, and then she invited me for dinner. Speaking of which, that's why I was late. She's a really nice girl. I think you would like her."

For a moment, Lee thinks his mother is going to start shouting at him with her feeble voice. Instead, the corners of her eyebrows upturn into a saddened expression, and she says, "Please stop this, son. Please stop doing this. Just leave the poor girl alone, please."

That angers Lee. He's hardly even said a word, and she's already making assumptions about him. Can't she, just for once, be happy for him? Be supportive?

But no, it was easier for the bitch to attack Lee the moment he steps through the door. No wonder he hardly spent time in the apartment.

"You know what? You're getting too upset, Mother. It's not good for your pressure. I think you need to cool off," Lee says.

He turns off the stove, walks up behind his mother, and pushes the wheelchair toward the closet.

"I'm going to tell the police about this, Lee." His mother sobs.

Lee stops rolling her and opens the closet, revealing the dark interior.

"No, you won't." He gets behind her, grabs the wheelchair by the handles, and leans into her ear. "Besides, no one would believe you anyway. You're just a crazy, old woman with dementia, anyway."

With that, he rolls her inside the closet. His mother doesn't scream or beg him not to do it. She stopped doing that a long time ago because she knows it'll make no difference. Now she just silently accepts her punishment.

Lee grabs the edge of the closet door. "You're also not getting any dinner tonight because you've put on a few pounds."

His mother cranes her neck to give him a look. There's no anger in those eyes, only a look that says her son is a lost case and there's no coming back. Somehow, it doesn't bring satisfaction to Lee. He would have preferred if she cried and begged him to let her out. She used to do it, but not anymore. It would seem it's time for new kinds of punishments.

Lee closes the closet door and looks at his wrist watch. He's already wasted enough time tending to his mother. He walks into his bedroom, approaches the wardrobe, and grabs the edge of it. He pushes it out of the way, revealing a big hole in the wall.

He grabs the flashlight off his nightstand, turns it on, and sidles into the hole. The beam of light slices through the darkness, revealing hanging cobwebs and flying specks of dust. It smells sour in here, but Lee is already used to the smell.

He walks through the passage inside the wall, ignoring the sounds coming from the adjacent apartments. It's usually the same.

In 406, the married couple talks to each other, with the wife doing most of the talking. She hardly takes pauses for breath. The husband can only be heard muttering words of confirmation like *mhm* and *yeah*. Sometimes, they watch TV. Inside this passage, it sounds a lot louder.

In 405, there's usually music that sounds like it's from the fifties playing. Lee has never seen the person living there. It could be a young guy imagining that he was born in the wrong era, or an elderly man reminiscing.

In 404, there's silence. A programmer lives there, and he's really quiet. Not even the sound of keyboards. Maybe he has one of those silent keyboards that muffles the noise.

Lee stops in front of the one-way mirror of 403 that he's installed there himself and turns off the flashlight. He won't need it right now. He's staring at the bathroom of the apartment with bated breath. His crotch is already tingling from the upcoming excitement.

The bathroom door opens, and Andrea walks inside. Lee's breath catches in his throat when she looks directly at him in the mirror.

It's only for the briefest moment because she then proceeds to put the clean clothes she's brought in on top of the washing machine. She can't see him, and he knows it, but it still makes him paranoid sometimes. If only she knew that Lee was only inches away from her, so close that he could almost touch her...

Andrea takes her shirt off, revealing the white bra underneath.

Yes, Lee exhales.

She throws the shirt into the laundry hamper in the corner of the room. She takes her pants off, too. Her rear is round and pert.

The bulge in Lee's pants starts growing. He rubs it over the fabric, and it gives him immense pleasure. He's imagining groping Andrea's ass, rubbing his manhood on it...

Andrea runs the water in the tub, and while it's filling up, she walks up to the sink and faces the mirror. She's staring at herself, but to Lee, it looks like she's staring at him. He loves moments like these because he feels so close to the person in the bathroom. It's as close as they get to being intimate right now.

It's tempting, insufficient, but enough to make him reach into his pants and grasp his tool.

Andrea takes her bra off, revealing a pair of firm breasts with small nipples. Lee lets out a moan as he begins stroking himself. He instinctively sticks his tongue out and imagines licking those nipples until they're erect.

For a moment, Andrea pauses and looks around the bathroom as if she's heard Lee. It's impossible, though. Had there been complete silence, maybe she would have heard something, but she'd still be unable to pinpoint the source of the sound.

But with the running water in the background and the noise running through the pipes and the walls, there's no way she heard him, and that's why Lee confidently continues to masturbate.

He loves looking straight into her eyes as he strokes himself. He's imagining her looking at him doing it, and it turns him on even more.

Andrea takes her panties off. She's entirely naked. Lee's climax is building up. It's going to be an intense one, he can tell. He holds it off because he wants to enjoy this. When Andrea turns around to approach the bathtub, the sight of her rear bouncing with each step drives him over the edge.

He ejaculates four intense white ropes with a muffled moan just as Andrea turns off the faucet, engulfing the bathroom in silence. Lee presses a hand against his mouth.

For a while, he is left standing out there with his flaccid manhood between his legs, panting and staring at Andrea. He puts a hand on the mirror in an attempt to have physical contact with her. He wants to kiss her, to cuddle with her, to feel the warmth of her body pressed against his.

She's not aware of him. She's submerged herself in the hot water and lets out a small moan of pleasure.

Lee reprimands himself for not waiting a little longer because the sight of her naked body wet is even more divine than her just standing naked in the bathroom. He just couldn't take it anymore because she turned him on so much.

"I love you," he whispers to her.

If she hears him, she's not showing it in any way. She's in her own zone, lying in the bathtub with her eyes closed, letting the warm water wash away her exhaustion.

Lee stares at her a while longer and then puts his rod back in his pants and slinks back to his apartment.

Chapter 5

I sleep surprisingly well on the first night in my new place. I usually wake up at least once during the night because the temperature is uncomfortable to me or to go to the bathroom, but that doesn't happen here.

Either the bed is really good, or I was so exhausted that I fell into a coma.

When I woke up, I was covered in a film of sweat, though. The sheets and the pillow are drenched, too. It looks like the AC in the bedroom doesn't work. It's past 10 a.m., and I'm glad it's my day off. My body is still stiff from the unexpected physical exercises yesterday, and I feel like I could sleep more, but I'm the kind of person who feels guilty whenever I stay in bed so late. Sometimes, if I have a little too much free time, I start to worry that I might have forgotten to take care of something important.

By the time I brush my teeth and make breakfast, I receive a call from Becca. Probably wants to check up on me and see how I've settled in.

"Good morning," Becca says.

"Hi," I reply, my voice still a little croaky from sleeping.

"How was your first night in your new place?"

"Good. The bed is huge and comfortable. Not like in Ryan's apartment. My neck and back hurt all the time from sleeping there."

For the first few months of us living together, I loved the fact that Ryan and I were practically forced to snuggle up in bed because of how small it was. Later on, it became a burden. Either it became too hot, or I felt like I was being pushed all the way to the edge of the bed while he got to hoard the rest of it.

"Did you manage to get all the things inside safely?" Becca asks.

"Yeah, my landlord helped me with it," I say.

"The handsome guy? Look at you. You're already making friends on your first day."

I roll my eyes. "He was just helping me."

And we just happened to have a meal together afterward.

The conversation with Lee still rings in my head. Inadvertently, my mind replays it on repeat, focusing on certain moments. Moments that felt like there was some chemistry between us.

But I don't tell Becca any of that. She would immediately become too intrigued and ask me a ton of questions about whether I like Lee, if I felt anything brewing between us, and so on. I don't blame her. She's just curious because I'm her friend, but she also wants me to put Ryan behind me as soon as possible and start dating someone new.

There's no better way to forget someone old than by dating someone new, she said multiple times, and even followed that rule.

Either way, I'd rather avoid questions and suggestions from her for now.

"Jacob and I should have helped you with the move," Becca says.

"It's fine. You two were too busy, and I didn't want to bother you," I say as I take a sip of coffee.

My phone buzzes. I put Becca on speaker as I check who the message is from.

"We're never going to be too busy to help you with that," Becca says. "Jacob is going to complain about it, sure, but he complains about everything. You already know that by now."

But I don't respond because I'm staring at my phone's screen, reading the message.

It's from Ryan.

I knew it. I knew he would contact me. I just didn't think it would happen so soon. Couldn't even wait to get drunk, seriously?

I'm suddenly overcome not just by fear, but also a sense of pride. Nothing inflates a woman's ego more than a man running after her once he realizes he screwed up.

Still, this is trouble. A lot of trouble. Just seeing a message from him puts me back to the past, meaning it's going to take forever for me to heal. Why didn't I block him when I had the chance?

Some of your things are still here. Want me to bring them over to Becca's place? the message says.

"Hello?" Becca says.

"Yeah, I'm still here. Sorry, what's the last thing you said?" I ask.

"I said we're never too busy to help you. And if you happen to need something now that you've moved in, call me."

"Mhm," I mutter, but my eyes are still stuck on Ryan's message.

A bevy of thoughts is running through my head. Is there a hidden meaning behind Ryan's message? Does he want to use "your things are with me" as an excuse to see me?

The last time we spoke, he told me he didn't want me to leave. I almost didn't. I almost said screw it and started unpacking my already sealed boxes.

He really looked like he was sorry things between us were over in such a way, but I knew staying with him would only loop me back into the unhappy relationship, and nothing would change.

When we live with someone for a long time, being with that person becomes a habit to us, and when the time comes to end things, we mistakenly think that we still love them because we're afraid of that big change.

For the past minute or so, I've been contemplating whether to respond to Ryan's message or just ignore him. I realize, if I ignore him, he might call me, and the last thing I want is to talk to him. Even seeing a message from him is unacceptable.

Keep them, I send the message to him, knowing full-well it's going to do nothing to stop him.

"Andrea. You're distracted. What is it?" Becca asks.

"Nothing."

"Andrea."

Of course, she sees through me even when we're on the phone. Subtlety is not my strong suit.

"Sorry. I just got a message from Ryan," I say.

"Well, he lasted longer than I thought he would." Becca lets out a chortle.

I can't help but laugh with her.

"What does he want?" Becca asks.

"He asked me if I want him to bring my stuff over to your place," I say.

"He doesn't know you moved, right?"

"Nope. How would he? We haven't spoken in a while."

"Okay, cool. Then tell him to bring your stuff to my place. He'll come expecting to see you, but he'll be in for a surprise."

I let out another peal of laughter at that. I like Becca's idea. Maybe it's a mean thing to do, but Ryan is the one who's pushing to see me. I've told him already that I don't care about those things and he can keep them, but he keeps insisting.

It's not just that, though. It's a sort of petty revenge for making me lose years of my life with him. There are so many things I could have done in those two years, so many other people I could have met. I could have already been married and planning for a kid.

Instead, I have to do the whole dating thing from scratch, but not before going through the mourning process. Ugh.

"Well, too late. I already told him to keep the things," I say.

But before I even finish that sentence, another message pops up from Ryan.

I really think you should have them. Besides, I can't stand to see them here. I'll bring the things over to Becca's today.

"Actually, you know what? I think I might do that," I say. "I'll let him bring the stuff to your place. I mean, he's not going to let me go until I get those things back."

Fine. I don't care, I type.

"He's not going to let you go either way," Becca says. "Even if you agreed to meet with him and he dropped off your things, he'd find another reason for you two to see each other."

I sigh. "Breakups suck."

"Just ignore him long enough, and he'll stop chasing you. Guys are like that."

"Then you don't know Ryan. Him being persistent is how we started dating in the first place."

Becca sighs. "Just ignore him, girl. Because, the moment you decide to see him, you're going to give him hope. And you're also going to give yourself hope."

"I'm not going to give myself hope."

"That's what you think. But you're still vulnerable."

I don't disagree with Becca. What if she's right?

I don't know how I would react to Ryan if I saw him now. Would I look into those eyes and see a stranger or years of familiarity and shared intimacy?

I'm a firm believer that people who've had a history with each other have no business being in the same room again. Ryan had suggested after the breakup that we remain friends, but I wouldn't hear it. That would have been hell. Not only would things be awkward between us, but imagine if one of us met someone new.

God, just the thought of having to meet his new girlfriend, or worse yet, me meeting him with my new boyfriend and watching his world shatter into a million pieces makes me sick to my stomach.

I say to Becca, "Well anyway, he'll be there today. Please don't tell him where I live. Otherwise, he'll never leave me alone," I say.

"What do you take me for? Of course I won't tell him." Becca snorts. "But I think you should consider blocking him. I mean, why do you even still have him in your contacts?"

"In case something important comes up."

"Like what?"

"I don't know, Becca. We lived together for two years. There really could be something important I forgot there or whatever."

"If it were important, you would have remembered it already. And if it did happen that you forgot something at his place, I'd send Jacob to fetch it for you. Plain and simple. But please stop kidding yourself that you're keeping him unblocked because of that."

I should feel offended, but I'm not because Becca is speaking the truth. As much as I hate to accept it, a part of me is hoping for a change. I don't know what kind, but I'm hoping for it. It would need to be an astronomical, miraculous change, though, and that's not going to happen.

That's the reason why we broke up in the first place.

"Okay. You know what? You're right. You're freaking right," I say.

Without giving it a second thought, I go into my contacts and block Ryan's number, I also block him on all social media. I already deleted him from my friends and followers, but that's not enough.

"There. He's blocked everywhere," I say.

For a moment, I'm left feeling numb. How has this happened? Have I really just blocked Ryan, the man who was the number one person in my life? I fear I might have a relapse and unblock him, that's how uncertain I feel, but Becca's voice interrupts that confusion.

"I'm proud of you, girl. Listen, I have to head to work. If you need anything, I'm here, okay?"

"You already helped me a ton by letting me stay with you and Jacob. I hope I can repay you for that someday."

"Don't be ridiculous. That's what friends are for."

"Thanks. And hey, you and Jacob should come by these days to see the place."

"Will do."

When we hang up, I look around the big apartment and feel, for the first time in a long while, a pang of loneliness. It only now hits me: I live alone. Every night after work, I'll be coming back home to an empty and quiet apartment. On the weekends, I'll be watching our... *my* favorite TV shows alone.

Alone.

The thought makes me sad, and I suddenly feel tears welling up in my eyes. I squeeze my eyes shut and take a few deep breaths, because I'm determined to remain optimistic about my new life.

I decide to go out for a little bit, explore the neighborhood, maybe find if there's a park nearby, maybe a doughnut place.

I lock the apartment behind me and call the elevator. It's already descending from the ninth floor before I even press the button. When the elevator reaches floor four, it skips it and continues descending.

The family from the ninth floor must have taken it, and it's probably going to get all the way down to floor B1 like Lee had mentioned the night before.

Oh well. The stairs it is, then.

I walk past Lee's apartment and give it an aloof glance, but then I stop when I hear a voice inside. If it were Lee's voice, I would have continued walking without stopping for a second, but the voice I heard sounded feminine and elderly.

Is it possible that I've heard it coming from a different apartment?

As if to confirm my suspicions, the muffled voice comes again, louder this time. It sounds distressed. I really shouldn't eavesdrop, but my curiosity gets the better of me.

I tip-toe closer to the door and listen. I can't make out what the woman is saying. The air is intermittently plunged into silence between her bouts of shouting.

"No! I don't want to!" the voice says.

I think I hear a much softer voice responding to it, but it's so faint that it might as well be the sound of pipes or the elevator's whirring.

"No!" the elderly voice repeats a few more times.

Then, there's silence.

Then, I hear the lock of the door clicking right in front of my face. Lee is coming out!

I quickly spin on my heels and stride toward the stairs. I only manage to run two steps before I hear the door opening. That's when I resume walking normally to avoid arousing suspicion. I turn around just like every normal person would if they heard an apartment door unlocking on the floor where they live.

Lee is stepping outside and locking the door behind him. Our eyes meet, and he offers me a smile.

"Hi," he says.

"Hey," I greet back.

"How'd you sleep?" he asks.

The amicable attitude tells me he doesn't know I was eavesdropping.

"Amazing. That bed is something else."

"I picked that one out myself. The quality of the mattress is really important. I can't fall asleep unless it's hard enough."

"Great. Oh, one thing, though."

"Sure. What is it?"

"I think the AC in the bedroom doesn't work."

"No worries. I can stop by later to fix it if you're not too busy."

"Sure. Why not. I think I'm free later today."

Lee walks up to the elevator and calls it.

"Don't bother. The ones from the ninth floor have taken it," I say.

Lee groans in annoyance. "They're really getting on my nerves."

"Hey, Lee? I have a question," I say.

"Sure, Andrea. What's up?"

"Does a senior woman live on this floor?"

I don't want to tell him yet that the voice sounded distraught. I shouldn't worry Lee if there's no need for it. For all I know, I'm just overreacting.

The question seems to surprise him because his smile drops. "No, why do you ask?"

"It's just that I heard a voice that sounds like it belongs to an elderly lady."

"A voice that sounds like it belongs to an elderly lady?" Lee raises his eyebrows.

It's weird that Lee doesn't know about any elderly women living on this floor. That's why I convince myself I have all the more reason to tell him what I heard.

"She sounded distressed," I say.

"Oh!" Lee snaps his fingers. "You probably heard the woman from 401."

"No, it wasn't her. This sounded clearly like an old woman."

Lee considers my question for a moment, a pensive gaze plastered to his face. A moment later, he snaps his fingers and says, "Right, I forgot to tell you that sounds do tend to travel through the building here."

"Really?" I ask.

"Yeah. You might hear something from another floor traveling to this one. I sometimes even hear stuff in my own apartment."

"Oh. I didn't realize that."

"Yeah. It can get annoying at times, but you'll get used to it. Won't even notice it after a while."

"I was just surprised is all because I remember you telling me who lives on this floor, and none of the residents you mentioned was an old lady."

"Don't worry about it one bit."

I feel a little better now that we've cleared the air.

"It's funny because it sounded as if the woman's voice was coming from inside your apartment." I let out a chuckle.

But Lee doesn't laugh at that. The corners of his lips are vaguely curving into a ghost of a smile.

"I'm sorry, did I say something wrong?" I ask.

"No, I just can't remember if I turned off the stove, so I should check that out."

He pulls out his keys and sticks them in the keyhole.

"So, I'll come by later today, and if you're available, I'll check that AC for you," he says as he unlocks his apartment.

"Sure, Lee," I say and give him a small wave as I go for the stairs.

As I'm descending, I can't stop thinking about my interaction with Lee. He became weird toward the end, and I wonder if I should be worried about him.

By the time I'm out in the fresh air, I forget all about it.

Chapter 6

Lee waits until Andrea is out of sight before opening the door and stepping inside the apartment. He barrels into the living room and stops abruptly in front of his mother.

The old woman doesn't even see him at first, so she's startled when he stoops toward her and grabs the armrests of her chair

"All right, listen here, Mother. Things are going to have to change," he says, biting down on his anger. "No more shouting. You hear me? That nice, new girl that's renting my apartment heard you, and she almost figured out it was coming from in here. So, you're going to need to lower your tone, or I'm going to keep you locked in the bedroom. Got it?"

The old woman stares up at him with a mixture of confusion and fear. Does she even understand what he's saying? Sometimes, he thinks—he hopes—her mind is gone, but then her facial expression miraculously changes and she displays intelligence.

"Do you understand?" he asks again, emphasizing each word slowly.

She stares at him blankly a moment longer then nods.

"Good. You can continue watching the TV while I'm gone, but it'll be with a low volume."

Lee waits for the woman to disagree or shout at him. He hopes it will happen so he can lock her in the closet again. He's disappointed when his mother's response is silence.

"Did you hear what I just said?" he asks.

"Yes," the woman croaks.

"Aren't you going to thank me for allowing you to watch TV while I'm gone?"

His mother has been staring at her lap until then. She cranes her neck toward him, and Lee can tell by the saddened look in her eyes that his provocations have worked and that she's about to start crying.

"I think so often about your father lately, sweetie," she says. "I think about the days when you were still a child and how your father and I raised you. I wonder if there was anything we could have done differently."

Lee is smiling the whole time, enjoying the torment on her face. For a mother, there's no greater punishment than to know she's failed as a parent. Lee is a terrible son, and he openly admits that, but he is not a bad person, and no matter what his mother says, she would not convince him of it.

She continues, "But then I realize nothing could be changed. You are as sick as your father was. I saw it in him early on. Even before we got married. His eyes would drift to other women in the street, and I would see a look of lust there. Even worse, an obsession. But I didn't know it at the time. I just thought he was unhappy with only me."

Lee crosses his arms, curious to know where this story leads. His mom has never told him much about his dad, but suddenly, Lee wishes he could have gotten a chance to know the man. He feels like he could have learned a lot from him.

More importantly, he feels like he would get some understanding from him, something he never had in his life.

His mother says, "He would come home late and say he was working overtime, but when I called his office, they told me he never stayed late. I started to think he was cheating on me. I was sure of it. One day, I found pictures hidden inside the drawer of his garage. Dozens of pictures of a naked woman. I had proof he was cheating on me, but I didn't want to confront him just yet. So one night, I followed him. I followed him and what I saw…"

She puts a hand over her mouth and her red-rimmed eyes fill with tears. She shakes her head as if staving off nausea.

"What I saw…" Her voice cracks this time, so she takes a deep breath. "He was standing in the bushes, looking through a woman's bedroom window. His pants were around his ankles, and with the other hand, he was… Oh God." She sniffles. "He followed that woman home, and… He wasn't just stalking her. The pictures… They were taken from inside her bedroom while she was sleeping."

Lee's mother sobs for a little bit. Lee doesn't do anything to console her. He's disgusted by her for talking about his dad like he was some sort of monster. He never hurt that woman. He was observing her from a safe distance, and Lee's mother made it seem like he was a psychopath.

"I was pregnant with you at the time. Two months. When he saw me in that bush, I ran home. I was so shocked and didn't know how to process it. But I knew I had to leave him. I didn't want to raise a child with someone like that. So, I packed. But when he got home, he begged me not to leave."

"And you stayed," Lee says.

"I stayed because I saw remorse on his face. He even cried. I had never seen your father cry before then. So, I stayed. I gave birth to you. We were happy. You were everything to us. But then your father started to become absent from work."

Lee's mother shifted in her seat.

"There were other women. I only knew about the few, but I suspect there were more. I threatened to leave and take you with me, but he knew I was bluffing. I was unemployed, and I had nowhere to go. And I didn't want to just up and leave you with such a monster. There was nothing I could do. So, I made the terrible mistake of turning a blind eye to his obsessions. Later, he no longer even tried hiding it, and I stopped asking."

"It's your own fault for not leaving him when you had the chance."

"You're right. It's my fault, Lee. There were so many things I would have done differently. But if I could choose only one, I would throw myself down the stairs when I got pregnant with you, and the world would be a better place."

The smile on Lee's face is gone. He underestimated the old woman. She is still able to hurl devastating insults in his direction. No matter how many times he's heard it, it's still painful to hear such words from his own mother, the one person who is supposed to love him unconditionally, no matter what.

Screw her. He doesn't need her love.

Also, this insult works in his favor because he now has a reason to punish her.

"I think you need a time-out, Mother," Lee says.

He rolls her into the bedroom and closes the door without a word. He locks it and bangs on the door with his palm.

"You think about what you've said, and I expect an apology when I'm back," he says.

He takes a look at the time. Five hours in the bedroom should teach her a lesson. If she needs to go to the bathroom and pees herself, she's going to get punished even more.

Chapter 7

It's a nice day, so I spend some time walking in the park and, later, shopping. I don't know this part of the town too well, so it's interesting to explore. It also helps me take my mind off unwanted things.

There are some nice, peaceful streets close to my new place, I have to say. It's not just endless concrete. There are rows of trees on either side of the street, and some fences are decorated with vines and floral patterns. The people who walk past me nod and smile and greet me even though I don't live there.

I like it very much. It's like the equivalent of the suburbs. It reminds of where I grew up before moving to college. Sure, I grew up in a house that was one hour away from the nearest town, but the atmosphere was the same—peaceful and friendly.

By the time I come back home, it's already afternoon and I'm exhausted. I have over twelve thousand steps. On a normal day, I get maybe eight thousand. Nine or ten if I do the chores around the house.

I kick the shoes off my painful feet, plop onto the bed in the bedroom, and I whip out my phone to see a message from Becca.

Ryan stopped by. You should have seen the look on his face.

Next to the message is an emoji of a laughing face with a hand over the mouth. I laugh at that.

Did he ask where I live? I send the message.

Take a guess.

He did. Didn't he? Did you tell him?

Of course not. He said it was really important and that he needed to talk to you.

I'd hate to say it, but I'm enjoying the knowledge that Ryan is running after me like this and making a fool of himself. I bet he even tried to call me. When that didn't work, he probably tried contacting me on different platforms. Too bad because I've blocked him everywhere.

It feels so good to be in such control. It feels like ages since I've had that feeling. I'm so happy with it that I don't care if it's wrong or not. I hold onto it for dear life because it makes me feel good, and I really need those good feelings right now.

Every girl needs an ego boost every now and again.

LOL, I type to Becca and add a sideways laughing-crying emoji. *I hope he finally takes a hint.*

He won't, Becca responds. *Come on, Andrea. Do you really know him so little? He's gonna find a way to contact you.*

He can't contact me anywhere. I blocked him. Remember?

Oh, he'll find a way to get to you. He's persistent. That's what I'm worried about.

Why are you worried about that? He and I are done.

It takes Becca a little while to respond to that message. When she does, it simply says, *Yeah* with a smiley face next to it.

An unreasonable pang of anger surges through me. I know exactly what Becca is thinking. She thinks I'll take Ryan back with open arms the moment he contacts me. Does she really think I'm that weak?

Then again, Becca has known me for a long time. She knows me better than I know myself sometimes. She knows I tend to have difficulty putting an end to things. Years ago, before I met Ryan, I dated a guy who I used to break up with every now and again before making up with him days or weeks later. This went on for about a year.

When it was our anniversary, Becca had asked, "Is that with or without the breaks?"

So in retrospect, I can't really blame Becca for thinking I'm still like that. But people change. I've grown. Yes, I miss Ryan, but I would never go back to him because I know things will never be the same for us.

Everything in your new apartment okay? she asks.

That prompts me to realize how hot it is in the bedroom. The AC above my head is taunting me, snickering at me.

Yeah. But the AC in the bedroom is broken, I say.

So? Have the landlord fix it for you. There's your excuse to see him again, she adds a winking smiley face.

I'll talk to him about it. He was supposed to come by today, but he's not here. Anyway, you and Jacob should come by these days.

When?

This weekend?

Okay, deal.

The heat in the bedroom has caused sweat to start breaking out on my skin, and I can no longer take it. I'm too lazy to get Lee to come fix it right now, so I instead go into the living room and blast the AC to the max. I hope the cold air can reach the bedroom and keep it cool at night.

A bit later, I order some food, watch TV and, in the evening, take a shower and go to bed. The entire time, I'm expecting to hear a knock on the door from Ryan. He's so persistent that I won't be surprised if he does manage to dig up where I live.

Thanks to the quality of the bed, I fall asleep fairly quickly despite the heat.

***

While she sleeps, Lee watches from the tiny hole he perforated in the bedroom wall.

She's sleeping in a bra and panties. Her smooth skin is covered in a film of sweat. The blankets messily hang off the side of the bed, revealing her body in full glory. It's precisely why he sabotaged the AC and failed to show up earlier today to fix it for her.

He'll have to take care of it very soon. He can make excuses only so long before Andrea either catches on or hires someone herself to fix it.

Occasionally, she stirs, changes the position, unable to fall asleep because of the heat in the room.

Lee doesn't do anything just yet. He just watches. He allows the tension in his pants to build up. His penis is jabbing against his pants, begging to be released, but he continues waiting. He's savoring the moment.

Andrea shifts again. The way she's lying sideways right now gives Lee a perfect glimpse at her perfect ass. Her panties are short and very revealing, and it makes the bulge in his pants unbearable. He can no longer wait.

He pulls his thing free and starts stroking it. He's not going to last longer than a minute, he can feel it. He so wishes he could cum on her ass. When he climaxes, it's even more intense than the last time. He's unable to stop the small moan that escapes his mouth.

Just in that moment, Andrea turns to the other side, and Lee can see that her eyes are open. She props herself on one elbow and looks around the room. She thinks she's not alone, but she can't pinpoint the source.

Moments later, she lays her head back down on the pillow and falls asleep. By then, Lee has already returned to his own apartment. In the morning, Andrea will be none the wiser that someone had been watching her the night before.

Chapter 8

I hardly slept last night because of the heat in the bedroom. I kept tossing and turning, and a persistent patina of sweat tickled my skin. At around 3 a.m., I took my phone and scrolled social media. It was around 5 a.m. when I finally became sleepy.

It was the rays of sunlight peering through the window that woke me up. I blink furiously, but I'm having trouble keeping my eyes open. I squint at the screen of my phone to see that it's 11 a.m.

"Ah, crap," I say, feeling guilty that I overslept.

The worst thing is that I feel like I could sleep even more. I force myself to get out of bed, but my body feels like it has weights strapped to it. It's the heat draining my energy. The moment I cross the threshold into the living room, I'm hit with a cold wave of air. It's very unpleasant, and more importantly, it makes me angry that the living room AC seems to have this ability to freeze the living room without bleeding into the bedroom.

If Lee doesn't fix the AC today, I'm going to have to sleep in the living room tonight. In fact, I decide I'm going to talk to him right after breakfast. I have food in the fridge, but I don't feel like cooking. Either it's depression due to the breakup, or I've gotten too lazy ever since I took a few days off from work.

Either way, I tell myself it's fine to take a break for one more day. I go back to work tomorrow anyway. I get dressed and head out to the nearest Starbucks. I find a seat and spend almost an hour there munching on a lemon cake and sipping latte.

Even while dating Ryan, I sometimes went to coffee shops alone. I enjoy the sight of people coming in and out for their daily dose of caffeine before tackling the day ahead of them. I enjoy listening to the murmurs of the crowd and the lighthearted conversations in passing. I like the sound of cars passing by outside.

Most of all, I enjoy the invisibility. I can curiously observe people go about their business and no one would even look in my direction. Hell, I could even do something weird like start singing and no one would look at me.

I guess most of them have been living in a big city for a long time. I myself have been living here for a long enough time, but I guess roots aren't easy to snip. Having been born and raised in a small town, I tend to still exhibit some of those traits.

My dad always used to say: *You can chase a hillbilly out of the hills, but you can't chase the hills out of a hillbilly.*

I think that even after a few decades of living in big cities, I'll still have that echo of small town in me. Who knows? In the future, I might move back to a calmer place. Now that I have nothing—no one—holding me back, the sky is the limit.

My phone starts ringing. It's an unknown number, so I ignore it. If it's something urgent, they'll leave a message. I watch the screen until the ringing stops and the phone locks itself. I take a look at the number, but it doesn't mean anything to me.

Just then, the number calls me again. I groan and put the phone on the table. I let it ring again until it stops. When it calls the third time, I can no longer ignore it. What if it really is something important? I have no idea what could be so important that someone needs to call me three times, but it's gotta be a big deal.

So, I make the mistake of picking it up.

"Hello?" I say.

First, there's silence. And then I hear a voice. An all-too familiar voice that makes me regret picking up.

"Andrea, don't hang up, please," Ryan says.

I do exactly that. I hang up before I can process the action properly. My heart is thumping in my chest. My hands are shaking. The crowd around me suddenly dissolves into nothingness and the only thing that exists in the world is my phone.

And then it starts to ring again.

I press the red button to hang up and then quickly block the number. A part of me expects it to ring again, which it doesn't, of course. It's already too late by then. I've already lost my appetite and the latte tastes like dirt to me.

I'm too distressed to even recycle them. Instead, I hastily pick up my things and storm out of the place. The whole time while I'm walking down the street, I feel as if I'm being watched. The veil of invisibility that I'd enjoyed is gone. I don't stop to scan the crowds. There are far too many people for me to try and locate Ryan.

As I near my building, I keep wondering why he's so persistent. I curse under my breath, and the little control I felt like I had is gone, leaving me with a feeling of vulnerability. He can't keep doing this to me. I started to get better, and he's holding me back. He's holding both of us back.

I'm so angry at him I want to unblock him, call him, and scream at him to leave me alone. But I wouldn't accomplish anything with that. I'd only be hurting myself by lingering. I'll keep him blocked and if he calls me from another number, I'll block him there, too.

Even the most persistent guys have a limit. He's going to give up. I just have to be more stubborn than him.

I keep thinking about Ryan's call even when I take the elevator up to my floor—surprise, surprise, Samantha from floor nine isn't occupying it. I keep thinking about Ryan's call even as I insert the keys into the lock, even as I hear Lee calling to me.

"Oh, Andrea. Do you have a moment?" he asks.

"Yeah. Sure. What is it?" I ask absent-mindedly.

He walks up to me. "About the AC. Sorry, I couldn't make the time yesterday, but I'm available now. Want me to take a look at it?"

On the one hand, I really want to be alone with my thoughts right now. I don't want Lee noticing that something's wrong and asking me about it. On the other hand, being alone right now feels terrifying. I don't want to overthink and come to crazy conclusions about what Ryan might do next.

"Yeah. Now would be great," I say through a forced smile.

***

I find it attractive that Lee's so good at fixing things. He's handling the AC with ease while making small talk with me. I offered him a drink, but he refused, said fixing the AC would only take a few minutes.

"How do you like the neighborhood?" he asks while rotating a screwdriver.

"I love it. It's very calm. Reminds me a little bit of where I grew up," I say.

"Oh yeah? And where's that?"

"I come from a small town in the Midwest. No one really knows about it."

"So what made you move here?"

"I went to college nearby, and then I got a job here, and... here I am."

"It's a big change, though, isn't it?"

"It is, but I like it. I needed a different kind of pace, you know? Something faster than the stillness back home."

Lee lowers the screwdriver, wipes his hand on his shirt, briefly looks at me, before focusing his attention on the AC again.

"You ever miss it?"

"Sometimes I wish I could turn off all this noise in the city. But I kinda got used to it."

"Have you been to Williams Café yet?" he asks.

"No. What's that?"

"It's a nice little café just two blocks from here. It's actually soundproof, and it's not aloud to be too noisy in there, so if you ever want to experience the quiet again, I suggest going there."

"Williams Café? I'll have to keep it in mind."

"I could show you, if you like."

The sentence catches me off guard.

Smooth. Real smooth, Lee.

I'm glad he's not looking at me because I'm smiling. There's no way I can say yes to that, though. I have way too much going on, and I don't want to lead Lee on. I definitely like him, but I'm not in the right headspace right now to consider going on a date, even though I'm *very* tempted.

"What about you? How long have you been here?" I ask in a weak attempt to change the topic.

"All my life. Got lucky enough to get into college in the city and find a job right here. But I gotta be honest, the older I get, the more I consider moving to the countryside."

"Really?"

"Yeah. Big cities are great, but I think they're mostly for people who like to experience the speedy life. After a while, you want to settle down, take it slow."

"Never too late to do that."

Lee shrugs. "I guess not. But right now, life's too busy for me to consider that. I definitely don't want to stay here forever, though. I'd like to have a house with a view on forests and hills. I'll take nature over this concrete maze any day. I try to drive away from the city as often as I can, but it's way too far and I work a lot, you know?"

"It sounds like you'd love living where I grew up. We had a view of the mountains right from my backyard."

"Well, now I wanna know even more about your mystery hometown."

I laugh, but I don't tell him, mostly just to be a tease.

"How's the fixing going?" I ask.

"Good. Something inside got loose and was stopping it from working, but it should be okay as soon as I put it back together."

"Thanks for doing this, Lee."

"Oh, don't mention it. It's my duty as a landlord. Anything that breaks down, you let me know and I'll be here to fix it."

Well, I'm on the verge of breaking down. Maybe you can fix me, I jokingly think to myself.

"I appreciate it," I say.

He puts the AC back together, points at the remote, and says, "Give it a spin, won't you?"

I press the power button. The AC beeps, the grilles open, and cool air starts blowing.

"Easy peasy," Lee says as he gets down from my bed. "Sorry for walking all over your bed."

"Don't be silly."

"Everything else okay in the apartment?"

"Yes. It's perfect. Thanks again, Lee. Oh, and thanks for the café recommendation."

"You're welcome. You know where to find me if you need anything else."

I see Lee out. After that, I plop into bed and enjoy the cool gust produced by the AC. I spend the rest of the day being lay around the apartment, because why not? By evening, Ryan is no longer on my mind. I eat a peanut butter and jelly sandwich, prepare for bed, and go into the bedroom.

With the AC functional, I can sleep with the blankets on. I have trouble falling asleep uncovered, so this mixture of warmth under the blankets and coolness of the room temperature is perfect.

Weird, I know, but I don't see it any different than people who need white noise to fall asleep.

It isn't long before I drift into sweet, sweet dreamland.

***

At 2 a.m., Lee stands up from the couch and walks into the bedroom. He's been sitting in the darkness and silence since around midnight.

His mother is sleeping peacefully inside the bedroom. He quietly pulls the wardrobe out of place, which causes his mother to stir. He doesn't care if she's awake. She's seen him sneaking into the secret tunnel many times now.

The first few times, she warned him not to do it. When he didn't listen, she stopped trying to talk him out of it. Nowadays, she pretends she's asleep.

Lee grabs the flashlight off the nightstand and gives one final look to his mother. It's hard to tell in the dark, but he thinks her eyes are open and staring at him silently and judgmentally. He cracks a smile at her, one that says, "I can do whatever the hell I want, Mother."

The walk through the passage at night feels different. The building is asleep, quiet. Every small noise sounds different than during the daytime.

Lee likes coming here at night. It feels even more wrong, and that's what he likes about it. Forbidden fruit always tastes better. It reminds him of the early days when he just discovered his passion and started sneaking up to women's bedroom windows to watch them. The risk of getting caught always added to the reward.

He stops in front of the one-way mirror looking into Andrea's bathroom. It's dark and quiet. Nothing is moving.

Continuing on, Lee looks through the tiny hole he's perforated to look into the living room. The entire apartment is dark. Good.

Lee approaches the secret door he's built and unlatches it. He turns off the flashlight and is momentarily engulfed in complete darkness. His eyes adjust a moment later.

Slowly, he pushes the door, and it creaks open, revealing the dark interior of the apartment. Lee holds his breath as he scans the living room. He can hear the soft blowing of the AC. Good. It's going to mask any small noise he might make.

The apartment is clean. No dirty glasses anywhere. No leftover food. No mounds of clothes on the floor. Andrea is really tidy, it seems. Lee loves her even more for that.

He looks toward the bedroom. The door is open, and he hears soft and steady breathing coming from it. Andrea is asleep.

Lee tip-toes across the living room and peeks into the bedroom. There, he sees her, bundled under the blankets, sleeping peacefully. He walks inside and stops in front of her. He kneels next to the bed and stares at her.

She's so beautiful when she's sleeping. His urge to reach out to her, caress her face, run his hands through her hair, and kiss her is powerful. His breath quavers at that.

Why shouldn't he touch her, though? She's his to touch.

Lee's fingers inch closer to her face. They're trembling wildly.

Just as the tips graze Andrea's face, she gasps. Lee's fingers recoil. He's been expecting something like this to happen, so he's already underneath her bed, holding his breath.

He can hear Andrea shifting positions above him. The bed slightly creaks. Then, her feet dangle off the side of it, and she gets out of bed.

Lee presses his lips tightly in anticipation. He watches as Andrea's bare feet walk out of the bedroom, across the living room, and into the bathroom. He can't see her from here, but he hears a click and sees a sliver of light creeping into the living room.

Lee's heart is thudding loudly against his chest. If Andrea looks under the bed... Not only that, but if she looks toward the secret door...

The door was made to look like a wall, but Lee left it slightly ajar so he can return the way he came. It's the same blank wall she had asked him about when she first came for the apartment viewing.

He was too eager, too careless, and now he risks being found out.

He contemplates if he has enough time to run back into the secret passage and close the door. Before he can properly entertain that thought, he hears flushing in the bathroom, and the light clicks off. Lee stares unblinkingly at Andrea's bare feet as she approaches the bed.

She hasn't looked toward the secret passage. Good. Even if she had, it's dark. She wouldn't have noticed anything unless she really paid attention.

The bed creaks as Andrea sits on top of it, then Lee sees a pale light above that he realizes is Andrea's phone. Moments later, the light is gone. He hears the sound of the phone being placed on top of the nightstand.

There's a moment of silence before the phone loudly clatters to the floor.

Lee stares at the phone on the floor next to him. He's sweating profusely. Andrea lets out a small moan as she reaches down and fumbles to grab her phone. Her hand blindly feels the floor, inching closer to Lee's face. Her fingers touch the phone, she grabs it, and the hand is out of sight.

Andrea's feet disappear out of view, and the bed creaks some more as she shifts before going entirely silent. Lee breathes a tentative sigh of relief. He has the urge to suck in sharp breaths of air, but he can't.

Not before Andrea falls asleep. That might be a while, though.

He waits for minutes, close to an hour. He listens to her breathing. He knows how she sounds when she's trying to sleep versus how she sounds when she's fallen asleep.

When he hears her soft breathing again, he waits a few more minutes before he crawls out from under the bed. She's sleeping on her back and, as much as Lee wants to admire her beauty, he doesn't want any interruptions this time. He pulls out a syringe from his chest pocket and uncaps it.

Slowly, he lifts the blanket off of Andrea, exposing her thigh. He wants to caress and kiss that thigh so badly.

As gently as he can, he inserts the needle into her flesh. Andrea's breathing is interrupted by a soft moan. It doesn't matter if she wakes up now. She won't remember any of this in the morning anyway.

But she doesn't wake up even when Lee administers the sleeping drug.

He takes out the needle, puts the cap back on, and slides it back into his pocket. Now he doesn't need to be so quiet anymore.

He sits on the edge of the bed and gently runs his hand down Andrea's soft cheek. He's overcome with his love for her and can no longer contain his urge to kiss her. He leans closer to her and gently plants a kiss on her lips.

It only makes him want more.

He kisses her more vigorously, running his hand down her neck and toward her breasts. He's waited for this moment for too long. He can't wait any longer.

He flings the blanket off, revealing Andrea's sleeping gown.

"I love you, Andrea," he says as he starts unbuttoning his shirt.

Sometime later, when he's done, he creeps back into the secret passage and closes the door. Since no one sees him entering through the passage, no one will ever think to check that wall.

Chapter 9

I sleep so much better now that the AC is working. In fact, I sleep so well that, by the time I open my eyes, the sun's peering through the window, blinding me—again. That's not good. I fumble around the nightstand until I find my phone and squint at the screen.

"Shit," I say aloud and hop out of bed.

It's past 9 a.m., and I'm late for work. I always set up two alarms, five minutes apart, just in case I miss the first one. How did I manage to sleep through both of them?

I don't have time to worry about it as I put on my clothes and dial my manager's number. I had two missed calls from him, and he must be really pissed. He picks up as soon as it starts to ring.

"Andrea, where the hell are you?" he asks.

"Dwight, I'm so sorry. I don't know what happened. I must have been exhausted from the move," I blurt while I'm putting on my socks and squeezing the phone between my ear and shoulder.

"I don't care, just get your ass over here. The partner is already here, and he's not happy," he says.

"I'm on my way. I'll be there in fifteen minutes."

I catch myself wondering if that's the truth or not. The office where I work is around fifteen minutes away, yes, but I'll need longer than that to get there if I count getting dressed, grabbing my things, and getting out of the building.

I'm feeling really groggy, and a cold shower would have been really nice, but there's no time. I don't even have time to brush my teeth. I just put my clothes on, make sure my face and hair are sufficiently presentable, and grab my keys, phone, and wallet.

As soon as the apartment is locked behind me, I run to the elevator and press the button to call it. It starts descending from the ninth floor and I'm skipping from foot to foot while I impatiently wait for it to arrive.

Once the doors open, I propel myself into it.

Except, I stop the moment I see Samantha and her baby stroller occupying the entire elevator.

"Sorry, there's no room," she says coldly.

I don't even have time to protest before the elevator door closes. The thing is slow anyway, and the stairs are going to be faster. Still, I can't suppress the pang of annoyance that coats my temples as I run down the stairs.

I race down, and on the second floor, I remember that I forgot my wallet.

"Dammit!" I shout and spin around to climb back upstairs.

By the time I'm back up on the fourth floor, I'm out of breath and sweating. There's also a knot of nausea forming in my stomach. I'm not used to doing so much physical activity so frequently.

It takes me longer than I'd like to insert the keys into the lock and open the door. The more we rush, the more we fumble. The next problem I have is I can't find my wallet. I really, really should have taken a day off today, I realize at this point.

Not all bad days can become good, and this one has already started off pretty bad. A small part of me is telling me to call Dwight and tell him I'm not feeling too well and that I'll be staying in bed all day.

Really, I don't feel so good. There's a heaviness in my body that refuses to leave, and it could be just my imagination, but I swear that the nausea has gotten slightly worse.

"Come on, come on. Where are you?" I look around the places where I could have left my wallet.

The kitchen counter, the living room table, the bedroom nightstand, the pockets in my coat on the hanger…

Only when I put my hands in the pockets of the coat I'm wearing do I feel the leathery outline of my wallet sitting there. I could have sworn I checked there just moments ago, but I must not have been thorough enough, and those pockets are pretty deep and wide.

I double-check if I got everything I need on me, and once I'm sure I'm good to go, I step out of the apartment and lock the door. I check the time—I've already lost close to five minutes just looking for my wallet. I should have been on the subway already.

I'm at least lucky enough to have the trains run on time. While commuting, I'm able to catch my breath. The heaviness has finally left my body, but now it's my eyelids that have weight to them. I feel like I could go straight back to bed, but I don't allow myself to drift off. I have to be alert because my stop is coming soon.

When I arrive at the office after what feels like a trek from Shire to Mordor, my manager is standing in front, tapping one foot on the floor, his phone raised to his ear. When he sees me, he lowers the phone, puts it into his pocket, and ushers me inside.

There's a moment of intense silence while I wait for his reaction. I'm already bracing myself for a marathon of shouting.

"Where the hell have you been? Come on, he's in there," he says and points me in the right direction.

I apologize to him and start walking down the hallway.

"Andrea," he calls out.

I turn around to see what he wants.

"Take two minutes to freshen up. You look like hell," he says.

"I can't. I'm already really late for the meeting," I say.

"I'll tell the partner you'll be right there. Just… you just straighten yourself up, all right?"

He sounds like he's not saying what's really on his mind.

Either way, I listen to him and head into the ladies' room. As soon as I look in the mirror, I can tell what he meant.

"Yikes," I say aloud to my reflection.

My hair is disheveled, strands jutting in random directions despite me having tied it into a ponytail. Sweat glistens on my forehead, under my eyes, and on my neck. My nostrils are flaring as I still take quickened breaths from the physical exertion I subjected myself to.

"Take it easy, Andrea," I tell myself as I use a wet wipe to clean my face.

Thank God I don't have makeup on. Otherwise, the sweat probably would have smudged it everywhere and I would have looked like a hooker who just got off her shift.

I take longer than two minutes. I don't need that long to get myself cleaned up—us women have become efficient with those kinds of things—but I do need time to gather myself. I give a silent thanks to Dwight for giving me the extra time.

A few minutes later, I'm out and ready to meet the partner. He's a burly man in his fifties who makes eye contact only once before averting his gaze to his laptop. He nods at everything I say, but I don't feel like he's listening to me. It's impossible to tell if it's just his way of paying attention, or if there's scrutiny I'm being subjected to.

When I'm done giving him my proposal, he tells me he'll talk to his team, thanks me (which is when he makes the second and last eye contact), and leaves the office.

The moment I step out, I see Dwight standing there with his hands on his hips. He juts his head at me. "So?"

I hesitate to tell him the truth. I fear that if I disappoint him just one more time today, he's going to lose it.

"I... don't think things are looking good," I say.

"Oh, yeah? What makes you say that?"

"I don't know. I wasn't feeling it. I don't think he'll go forward with the contract."

"What did he say?"

"He said he's going to talk to his team, and that's it."

"Maybe that's exactly what he's going to do."

"Maybe. I would just be ready not to hear back from him again."

The easy thing would have been to lie to Dwight. To tell him that the partner seemed very interested and that we have a good shot. That way, I'd avoid any further backlash today. I'm not the kind of person that likes to take painful things one step at a time. I prefer ripping off the Band-aid and getting it over with.

As I stand there bracing myself for another reprimand, Dwight simply nods, his face slackens, and he says, "I see. Well, I'm sure you did your best despite the hiccup we've had. Anyway, I'm sure you have a lot of work to get back to."

I'm glad the conversation went so smoothly, but I can feel like Dwight is holding back his anger. Maybe saving it for when we don't hear from the partner so he can unleash his fury on me then. Or maybe he understands I've been through a lot lately, too.

I get back to my desk to work on my daily things. When work is done, I return home, exhausted about as much as I was when I finished moving all the boxes inside the apartment. I decide it's time to take another hot bath.

I usually prefer showering, but lately, I feel as though I really need a long, lazy bath. In fact, I need an entire spa day, so I consider booking one for the weekend.

I enter the bathroom and turn on the faucet, but no water comes out. I hear a squeak and a gurgle, indicating that the faucet is trying to unleash water, but nothing happens.

You've got to be kidding me.

Less than a week, and things are already breaking down in this apartment.

Well, I can't not take a bath, and Lee had told me that I can come to him in case I ever need anything fixed in the apartment. I'm hesitant to bother him so often, but then again, he's the landlord. It's his responsibility.

I'm not very happy about having to get dressed again so I can talk to him about this. I'm grouchy the whole time I'm getting dressed, but I try to put on a friendly face before heading to apartment 407.

Chapter 10

I ring the doorbell and wait for Lee to open. No one comes out. I ring again. I know the doorbell works because I hear a very loud *bzzzt* inside the apartment whenever I press it. I impatiently tap my foot on the floor.

I'm really annoyed right now. I should have been taking a hot bath already. Stupid, dysfunctional apartment that needs constant repairs. No wonder rent is so low. And where in the hell is Lee? Why isn't he opening the damn door?

As much as I don't want to admit it, I've brought residual anger back from work. Realizing that, I force myself to calm down. I don't want to take my anger out on Lee. He's a really good guy and he's been nothing but kind to me. I'd feel guilty if I burned that bridge.

Finally, I decide to knock on the door, refusing to believe Lee isn't home. The moment my knuckles connect with the wooden frame, the door creaks open. When that happens, all my anger is gone, replaced by curiosity.

Startled, I lower my hand and peek through the crack. I can't see anything because it's too dark. I stand frozen for a moment, contemplating what to do. This isn't really a situation I'm used to experiencing. Do I just walk away and pretend I didn't see anything?

Becoming more daring, I gently place the tips of my fingers on the door and slowly push. The door produces a loud creak as it stands ajar.

"Hello? Lee? Are you home?" I call out.

My voice sounds cracked against the pervading silence.

I push open the door further and call out to Lee once more. When he doesn't respond, I take one tentative step inside. I know I'm trespassing, but this is no longer just about the bathtub. It's about finding my landlord's apartment door not only unlocked but also open.

He could be in danger. It might be a matter for the police. I'd be selfish to pretend I didn't see anything.

"Hello," I say again as I step into the foyer.

It's dark in here, and I can just barely make out the outline of the walls and furniture in the living room—what I can see from here, anyway. The apartment shouldn't be this dark. There's still plenty of daylight outside, which means Lee probably has the blinds on the windows down.

"Lee? It's Andrea. Are you home?" I keep announcing my presence because I don't want him to think I'm a burglar.

No response.

I tip-toe forward, intermittently calling out to Lee. It feels like that old trick you use in the woods where you know there are bears—keep shouting to let the bear know to steer clear.

When I reach the entrance to the living room, I stop. I see Lee's outline seated in a chair in the middle of the room.

"Lee?" I call out.

He's sitting in darkness. Is he sleeping? His head seems ramrod straight, though, not slumping like it would to someone napping. It's disconcerting, because I can feel Lee's eyes on me. He knows I'm here, and he sees me, but he doesn't say anything.

A chill clambers down the nape of my neck along the length of my spine. I don't like this at all. I suddenly want to do an about-face, run out of the apartment, and pretend I never saw the open door. Screw the hot bath, I'll take it another day.

But I can't move. I'm frozen. That pair of eyes in the chair is petrifying me.

"Lee," I say, but my voice sounds timid even to me.

I rap on the wooden surface of a shelf next to me to get his attention. Nothing. I don't know why I'm still pretending like everything is normal when it's clearly not. Instinctively, I fumble around the wall to find the light switch and flip it on.

Immediately, a pale light washes over the room, and I face Lee.

Except, the person sitting in the middle of the living room is not Lee.

"Get out!" the old woman in the wheelchair shouts so loudly I scream and stumble backward.

My back hits the doorframe.

"Get out! Get out! Get out!" the old woman shrieks, each sentence louder than the previous one until it sounds like her vocal cords are going to snap.

"I'm sorry! Okay! I'm leaving! I'm so—"

Just as I turn around, I bump into a tall figure and let out another scream.

Lee is standing in front of me, a serious expression on his face that looks like he's about to scold me. Only when I realize it's him do I start to calm down.

"Oh. Lee. It's you," I say in relief and confusion.

His face is deadpan. I haven't seen him like this before, and it terrifies me.

"What are you doing in here?" he asks atonally.

"I wasn't... The door was open, and I... I came looking for you because there's something wrong with the bathroom, and..."

My excuses sound like just that. Excuses. I can also tell by the reticent stare on Lee's face that he's not buying it, so I slow down, take a deep breath, and start anew.

"Sorry. I rang the doorbell, I..."

"Get out of here!" the old lady yells behind me.

"...I was looking for you because there's something..."

"Get out!"

"...wrong with the bathroom, and I really need..."

"Get out! Leave!"

"...to take a..."

"Get! Out!"

Lee's eyes flitter from me to the living room, and I can tell he's stopped listening to me.

"Mom," he calls out and brushes past me into the living room with hurried steps.

"Get out!" the woman shouts.

She doesn't seem to be looking at me anymore. Her head is snapping left and right as she screams the same thing over and over. I enter the living room after Lee, and the woman's eyes focus on me once again.

"Get out!" she shouts, gripping the armrests of her wheelchair so hard that the thick veins on her hands are bulging like worms.

Meanwhile, Lee has walked over to the cabinet and opened a drawer. He's fiddling with something, and when he faces me again, there's a needle in his hand.

"It's okay, Mom," he says as he kneels next to her and administers the needle into her arm.

He's doing it so professionally that it makes me wonder how long he's had to handle medical equipment.

"Get out! Get out!" the woman is still screaming at me.

Seconds after the liquid enters her bloodstream, her *get outs* grow weaker, her eyes flutter, and her head slumps. Finally, she's asleep.

Lee kneels a moment in front of her while silence takes over. He then turns toward me.

"I'm sorry. I didn't mean to come inside," I say. "I saw that the door was open, and I was worried something might have happened to you."

First I had to explain myself to Dwight about being late, now to Lee about going inside his apartment. I had been right. Not all bad days can become good. I should have just stayed in bed.

I wonder if my leasing of the apartment is going to come to an end so abruptly because I trespassed into Lee's place. He smiles at me compassionately and stands up. That gives me some assurance that he understands.

"Don't worry about it. I would have done the same thing," he says.

We stand in awkward silence for a little while. I can't get my eyes off the old woman sleeping in the wheelchair. Her chest rises and falls steadily. It's difficult to imagine that this woman was screaming at me at the top of her lungs just moments ago.

"Your mother lives with you?" I ask.

I can't tell if I'm intruding with the question just as I intruded by entering.

"Yeah." Lee nods.

"Why didn't you tell me?"

He scratches the back of his head. "You said you have a problem in your bathroom, right?"

"Yeah. There's no water for some reason."

"Okay. How about I check that out for you?"

"You know what? I'll just call a plumber to have a look. You must be busy with your mother and—"

"Don't be silly. I'm the landlord; it's my job to fix it." He smiles, and the tension is gone just like that. I take it as a sign that he's not angry at me.

He gets behind his mother and rolls her into the bedroom. His head turns somewhere to the left and stays fixated on it for a moment. Maybe he's noticed something on the wall that needs fixing. I'm tempted to step after him to see what the problem is. Before I can do that, he retreats from the room and gently closes the door behind him.

"Let's take a look at your problem, huh?" he asks politely as we head out.

Chapter 11

"Do you think you can fix it?" I ask Lee.

I'm standing in the middle of the bathroom while he's using various tools to loosen up the bathtub's faucet and see where the problem is.

"Yup, not a problem," he says, his voice strained because his head is turned almost upside-down for him to look inside. "Just going to need a few minutes if that's not an issue for you."

"Not an issue at all."

Lee spends the next minute or so fiddling with the faucet in silence. I want to strike up small talk, but I have no idea what to say. Frankly, I'm still distraught from Lee's mother screaming at me. I can't get the old woman's face out of my head. I still hear her voice shouting *Get out*.

Lee must be thinking about the same thing because he says, "Sorry about my mom scaring you like that. She can be pretty terrifying when she has… um, her episodes."

I'm glad he's the one who opened that topic because now I have an excuse to ask the many questions that are on my mind.

"What's wrong with her?" I ask.

Lee doesn't look at me. He's focused on the faucet, but I can tell he's pretty much looking through it.

"She has dementia," he says. "It's pretty advanced. The doctors say she doesn't have too long to live."

"That's terrible. I'm so sorry to hear that, Lee."

I only know in theory what it's like to deal with a loved one suffering from dementia, and I know it's a very difficult situation. I don't even want to ask Lee how tough things must be for him.

"Well, what can you do," he says. "I didn't want to tell you anything about it because I didn't feel like getting into the whole story and explaining everything. I'm sure you can understand."

"Yeah."

I do. Lee doesn't need to justify himself to me. He's probably had people asking the same questions about his mom many times in the past, and he's sick of always explaining the same thing and getting the same shallow responses from people that say they're sorry.

He says, "Anyway, she needs attention most of the time, so I try to give it to her. It does get tough, though. Physically, she's pretty much okay, but mentally, her mind's gone. It's a terrifying thing. Growing old and becoming like my mother scares me a lot."

I want to approach him and gently touch him, tell him how sorry I am he has to go through that, because I don't know what else to say to make things better. Something's stopping me, though. Maybe the fact that Lee and I don't know each other so well yet.

Still, it's undeniable there's some kind of a spark between us. I think it's because we shared our vulnerabilities with each other and it sort of made us bond. I can feel it, and I wonder if he can, too.

In the end, I don't do or say anything because I don't want to get carried away. Lee being my landlord is not the only problem—and that in and of itself is already a huge issue.

The fact that I'm still getting over Ryan further complicates things. I reckon it's going to be a while before I start dating properly again. But that's only if I take into consideration that Ryan will hopefully leave me alone.

Lee assembles the faucet back to the way it was, turns it on, and it works. He looks at me with a proud smile as if to say, "Told you I could fix it."

"You're good at this," I say.

He turns off the water, stands, and wipes his hands against one another. "No big deal. I'm sorry you had to deal with this in the first place."

"I'm just glad you were able to get it fixed."

"Absolutely."

Lee puts the tools back in his toolbox and picks it up. For a protracted moment, we stand in front of each other without uttering a word, that spark from before back, electrifying the air in the bathroom.

It feels as though we're going to kiss if we stand like this for too long, and I decide to put a stop to it.

"Well…" I clear my throat. "Thank you again for fixing the tub, Lee. Now I can finally take that bath I've been waiting to take."

"Right. And I should get back. It's almost time for my mother to take her meds," Lee says.

"All right. Take care of her. She seems like a nice woman, despite the fact that our only interaction was her screaming at me."

"Unfortunately, her moments of lucidity are less and less frequent, so having a normal conversation with her is not very possible. I'm sure she would have liked you, though, if she were aware enough to, you know, get to know you."

I suddenly picture Lee and myself dating and me meeting his mother for a second time. I would try to talk to her, but she'd either give me a blank stare or do something completely unexpected again—like scream or squeeze my wrist.

I shove those thoughts away as I step aside to let Lee pass.

"If anything else breaks down, let me know, Andrea. I mostly work mornings, but I'm here the rest of the time, so don't hesitate to ask for help if you need it," Lee says.

"Thank you again," I say as I see him to the door. "I don't know how I can repay you."

"Don't worry about it. Have a great night."

He turns to leave, and I'm about to close the door when he calls out to me.

"Oh, Andrea? Actually, there is a way you can repay me. We never had those beers after we ordered food. I got a few cold ones in the fridge I bought a few days ago, so I was thinking, if you're up for it, maybe we could… you know… hang out one of these days."

I'm about to open my mouth to tell him I might be busy with work and all that—which is an excuse, by the way—but then he quickly interrupts me before I can speak up.

"Nothing committal," he says. "Just a couple of beers, that's all. As friends."

When he puts it that way, I don't see a reason to say no. He's been nothing but respectful up until now. I'm sure he's not going to do anything I'll dislike. He's my landlord after all, and it would make the situation between us uncomfortable.

"Sure. Sounds good," I say.

He flashes me a smile and walks back to his apartment. I close the door, and I realize that I, too, am smiling.

The rational part of me is telling me to stop fantasizing about me and Lee together, but the other part—the one that ignores logic and follows emotions—doesn't do anything to stop me.

I don't realize how aroused I am until I'm naked and in the bathtub, my hand between my legs. My eyes are closed, and I'm moaning as I imagine Lee doing things to me.

The pleasure is interspersed with jabs of pain, though, because in moments, it's not Lee who I imagine doing things to me but Ryan.

***

From behind the mirror, Lee watches Andrea touching herself. He touches himself along with her. He feels so much closer to her. The experience is almost as good as sex.

It takes her a while, but soon, she throws her head back and lets out a stifled moan. He synchronizes his masturbation so that he climaxes at the same time as her. He then spends a long time staring at her in the mirror, imagining running his fingers down her naked body, kissing her neck, whispering to her how much he loves her.

She's unaware of his presence. He's practically invisible, and it makes him feel like a god.

Chapter 12

Tonight, Becca and Jacob are officially coming to see my new place, so I stocked up on their favorite snacks. I decide I'll serve snacks instead of a cooked meal because I'm not a great cook. I also bought a bottle of wine. Just one, because Becca doesn't know when to stop. I also took extra care cleaning the apartment.

Two hours before their arrival, I pace from room to room and make sure everything is in order. Becca will want to see every room. An hour before their arrival, I take a shower and get dressed. This visit feels very formal, I suddenly realize. Like a business dinner.

I'm the only one who feels that way, I'm sure. Becca and Jacob are coming to see how I'm doing, not to inspect my apartment. The closer the time approaches, the more excited I get. It's been weeks since I've seen Becca and I'm really looking forward to it.

When the doorbell rings, I walk up to the door with a grin on my face, ready to scream at the sight of Becca and hug her while Jacob awkwardly stands there. I open the door, and there they are. Becca is holding a bottle of wine, something she probably brought as a housewarming present that would end up getting opened tonight. Jacob is standing behind her.

The two of them are overdressed for the occasion, and I suddenly feel like I should have told them not to make such a big deal out of this.

Becca leaps to embrace me in a tight hug. She lets out a small whimper of happiness, and just as I predicted, Jacob is left standing there waiting for us to finish holding each other. After that, I hug him, too.

"Come on, get in." I gesture for them to get inside.

The first few minutes are spent with them admiring the apartment. I let them go explore it, even though there's not much to explore. The living room is the highlight of the place, mostly because of its spaciousness.

I also have to say that my decorating of the apartment really gave it life. It was already nice when I moved in, but it was devoid of any personal touch—my touch. I like to come back from work and see things that belong to me. That way, I feel more like it's home and not just a place I'm renting.

"Wow, and this place is really that cheap?" Jacob asks.

"I couldn't believe it, either," I say.

Becca emerges from the bedroom. I expect to see a smile on her face but, instead, she looks pensive.

"What's the problem, Becs?" I ask.

"I'm just thinking there's gotta be a catch here," she says.

"Exactly what I thought, too. But there's no catch. The landlord is just really nice. He believes in helping people."

Jacob snorts. I look at him and it takes me a second to understand he's laughing at my statement. When he sees the grievous expression on my face, he says, "Sorry."

But then I look at Becca, and I can see a familiar look on her face—one that she has whenever she wants to tell me something but is unsure if she should.

"What?" I ask.

"It's nothing," she says. "Why don't we pop open the wine bottle?"

She's about to make her way to the couch when I stop her. "No, no, no. You're not telling me something. What is it?"

Becca and Jacob exchange a glance.

"I just think you might want to not trust your landlord so much," Jacob finally says.

"Why? You think he lied to me about something and that's why rent is so cheap?"

Becca says, "Andrea, people are generally selfish. I don't see why someone would rent an apartment out to a stranger for such a low price unless there was something faulty with it."

"Well, maybe I'm just lucky. Did you think about that? Maybe I ran into a good person who doesn't care about money," I say.

Honestly, the conversation is making me angry. I hate that instead of being supportive and happy for me, my best friend is skeptical. Am I being the unreasonable one here?

"You know what? You're probably right," Becca says. "Maybe Lee really is selfless. And if so, you got really lucky to find this place. I'm just glad to see you've settled in nicely."

I can tell she's just saying that to try and deescalate my anger. As angry as the conversation is making me, I don't want it to end like this. I want to have the last word, to tell them they're wrong about Lee and that this place is perfect.

Instead of making a scene, I smile and say, "I'll bring out the snacks. You two make yourselves at home."

Just then, the doorbell rings.

"Oh," I say, surprised.

"Are you expecting more company?" Becca asks.

"No. Just you two. Hold on a second."

I open the door to see Lee standing there.

"Lee, hi," I say.

He has a concerned look on his face. My immediate assumption is that something bad happened to his mom.

"Is everything okay?" I ask.

"I was about to ask you the same thing. Are you all right?"

He peers over my shoulder inside the apartment. I crane my neck at Becca and Jacob, who are watching intently. When I turn back to Lee, I say, "Yeah. Everything's fine."

"It's just that I heard a scream just a few minutes ago," he says.

"A scream?" I ask.

I hear Becca and Jacob's footsteps approaching me.

"Yeah, that was me. Sorry," Becca says. She outstretches a hand for a handshake. "I'm Becca, by the way."

"Hi. I'm Lee." Lee shakes her hand, and then Jacob's. "I didn't realize you were having guests over."

"Yeah," I say, then pause.

It suddenly dawns on me. What if that's the whole catch? That Lee doesn't want me to have any guests over?

Surely, that won't be a problem, will it? Surely, Lee expects I'm going to have company over from time to time, right? What kind of a crazy landlord would not allow that?

Lots. Lots of landlords are like that. I've read so many horror stories online about landlords from hell that I know things can get pretty crazy with some homeowners. Lee has been nothing but kind to me, but what if he has a list of rules he expects me to follow? He would have told me about that, right? Besides, he's told me multiple times to make myself at home.

"Sorry, is that going to be a problem?" I ask.

"What? No. Absolutely not," Lee says, shocked by my statement. "You can invite whoever you like. I just wanted to make sure you're okay."

"Yeah. Becca and I were just a little too happy to see each other again."

"Right. I understand. So, what are you guys doing tonight? A little catching up? A little drinking?" He winks at me.

"Sort of. Just talking, I guess."

I'm holding the edge of the door, ready to say goodbye to Lee, but I don't do it just yet. I'm waiting for him to tell me if he needs anything else. There's a moment of awkward silence as Lee stands at the door, as if still expecting something. I can sense the awkwardness transferring onto Becca and Jacob as they stand in silence.

"Well, thank you for coming by to check up on me," I say.

Slowly, I start to close the door to indicate the conversation is coming to an end.

"Don't mention it. You have a great time." Lee flashes me a smile.

Just before I close the door, he turns around and strolls down the corridor. Even when the door closes, the awkward silence still lingers in the apartment.

Becca and Jacob walk back to the couch. They're quiet while I get the snacks out. In minutes, though, the conversation between us resumes as if the interruption had never happened, and we have a great time.

The way Becca starts drinking is worrisome, but she stops herself after just two glasses of wine. I guess she's getting tired of reckless drinking as much as I am. We're not in our early twenties anymore where we could drink at someone's place as a pre-game and then go out and continue drinking until dawn.

Nowadays, we're responsible adults with jobs and a feeling of saturation toward partying. Occasional drinking is fine. Getting blackout drunk is no longer in our stamina capability.

"Hey, I didn't tell you. Ryan called me recently," I say.

"Seriously? How? Didn't you block him?"

"I did. He called me from an unknown number."

"Wow, what a pathetic loser."

"He really doesn't know when to give up."

Becca takes a sip of wine. "Well, just keep blocking him everywhere, and eventually, he's bound to give up."

"I just hope this was the last I heard from him."

"It's not. You know he's going to contact you again."

I don't like that, because I feel like every time he tries to get in touch, I'm thrown a few steps back. I don't want to go backward anymore. I want to go forward.

"Hey, but seriously, how are you doing regarding that?" Becca asks as she puts a hand on my wrist.

"I'm better. Really. It's still difficult sometimes, but I'm optimistic."

"Do you think you'll be ready to start dating soon again?"

"I'm not sure. Why? Are you gonna tell me I should hook up with my landlord?"

Becca looks away from me, into her glass of wine. "You should take things slow. Don't push yourself until you feel it's right."

"I appreciate you saying that."

It's well past 2 a.m. when Becca and Jacob decide it's time to go. I've had so much fun catching up with Becca that I haven't even noticed that time flew by so fast.

"Thanks for coming by," I say as I see them to the door.

"Of course. Love the place," Becca says.

We hug at the door, and they're about to leave, but then she hesitates.

"What's up?" I ask.

She cranes her neck to look down the hallway. "So your landlord lives in that apartment there, right?"

"Uh-huh."

"Cool."

But she continues staring at the door to Lee's apartment. Jacob is staring there, too.

"Is something wrong?" I ask. Then when I realize what they might be thinking, I add, "Look, having a landlord this close is not as bad as you think. He doesn't barge in or anything. He doesn't even check up on me. In fact, it's convenient because whenever something breaks down, he fixes it for me."

"Oh, definitely," Jacob says. "He seems like a cool guy and all. Becca and I just had bad experiences with landlords so we're a little skeptical, that's all."

"I get that, but Lee is really sweet and helpful. He's done nothing but make me feel comfortable ever since I moved in."

Why does it sound like I'm defending myself to Becca and Jacob? This entire night, I've felt as though they're not happy for me, but scrutinizing my new apartment, trying to find faults with it.

It dawns on me that maybe they're jealous I got this place so cheap. I mean, who wouldn't be?

"I'm glad you've settled in, Andrea." Becca hugs me again. "And you look so much better. I'm happy for you."

"Thank you. And thank you for letting me stay with you after breaking up with Ryan. If you and Jacob ever don't work out, you can crash in my place," I jokingly say.

Becca laughs, but there's no sincerity in that laughter.

We say goodbye and I close and lock the door. I'm supposed to be feeling accomplished, like I always do after a good hangout. Instead, the feeling is marred by something I can't define. It's a feeling evoked by Becca. By something she's not telling me.

For the first time in forever, I feel as though my best friend is not being honest with me, and I can't tell what it's about.

I'm too tired to worry about it, so I decide to do what I do best—ignore it and pretend it'll go away.

Chapter 13

I'm stopped in the middle of the office hallway by Dwight, which I'm not very happy about.

"You done with that report, Andrea?" he asks me.

I slow down but don't stop to let him know I'm in a rush to eat. "Almost. I'll email it to you right after my break."

I hate it when Dwight tries to talk to me during my lunch break. The one hour already feels too short, and I don't need my manager to keep reminding me I have to go back to work soon. The fact that I feel like crap today doesn't help one bit.

"Great. Make sure to CC Rachel," Dwight says.

"Okay." I nod, and I'm already well on my way to walk past him.

"Hey, one question."

Now irritated, I stop, turn around, and force a smile. "Yes?"

"Are you okay? You look tired. Get enough sleep?"

I've been groggy since morning despite having slept for more than nine hours last night. I drank two cups of coffee and one energy drink, it's past noon, and my body still feels like it weighs fifty pounds.

It's difficult to focus on work today, but I do my best. I can't afford any mistakes because we're getting a lot of work lately. Despite that, I can't get my bed out of my head. I can't wait to go home, slump into it without even changing, and take a long nap. I don't even care if I can't fall asleep tonight because of it. I'm going to sleep until this weight is completely gone.

"Yeah, I'm fine," I say, mostly because I don't trust Dwight enough to tell him I'm sleepy. If I do, he's going to ogle me suspiciously, and he'll scrutinize everything I do. That's the last thing I need right now.

I can see that Dwight is not happy with my curt response, so I quickly add, "I'm fine, Dwight. Really."

Dwight nods. "Okay. It's just that we're dealing with numbers, you know. One mistake could cost the company a lot. If you need help with your workload, ask Rachel, or you can let me know and I'll divide the tasks more equally."

"That won't be necessary. Thank you for your consideration, though," I say.

Sometimes, I become aware of how formal I sound in a workplace setting. Anyone who knows me outside of work would be able to tell how fake I sound in the office, and anyone who knows me at work would be surprised at the shift in personality outside my job.

I wouldn't call it fake. I'm simply adjusting to various environments. I like to think that means I'm versatile.

"Okay. Enjoy your lunch, and I'll be expecting your report shortly," Dwight flashes me a toothy grin. I don't reciprocate the smile when he turns around and leaves.

I never thought about it before, but he's probably as different outside of work as I am. For a moment, I wonder what he's like. Is he as annoying and controlling as he is at the company?

Prick.

I'm not normally this irritated, but the heavy eyelids are contributing to my annoyance. I pray for the day to be over soon, because I really don't want to snap at anyone.

Unfortunately, the day goes by very slowly, just as it always does when we're sleepy. To make matters worse, I make a mistake in my report and Dwight makes sure to reprimand me for it. Rachel is the one that fixes my mistake and sends the amended version to Dwight, making me look like an incompetent moron.

Today, I don't care. I already got a promotion six months earlier, and I don't care about chasing another one—not when the salary and working hour increase are so disproportionate. I just want to go home and sleep.

I don't waste my time when 5 p.m. comes. I pack my things and get out of the office. My head is slumping on the subway, but at least I have a spot where I can sit.

The elevator in my building is on the ninth floor, but at least nobody is using it. Thanks, Samantha Turner from the ninth floor. I lean my head against the wall and close my eyes while I wait for the elevator to descend. I then get the idea to check the mailbox for bills.

I pull out my keys, unlock the mailbox, and pull out the three envelopes stacked inside. The elevator opens just as I return to it, which I'm grateful for. I take it up to the fourth floor, unlock the door to my apartment, and enter.

As soon as I'm in, I lock the door behind me because I have no intention of going out anywhere today. I kick my shoes off, rifle through the envelopes, and...

I freeze in the middle of the living room, and I'm suddenly no longer sleepy.

Nestled between the envelopes was a folded slip of paper. I thought nothing of it as I opened it up to see what it is. Now, I can't stop staring at the simple message written on it in capital letters with a crude handwriting.

"LEAVE THIS PLACE," it says.

Chapter 14

My first thought is: *Ryan*.

As quickly as the thought manifests, it disappears. Ryan is persistent, but he's not evil. He wouldn't leave a message like this one to me because he knows how freaked out I'd be. If he knew where I lived, he would simply knock on my door.

No, this isn't Ryan's doing. So then, whose is it?

I can't stop staring at the piece of paper.

LEAVE THIS PLACE.

I suddenly feel like I'm being watched. A chill runs down my spine. I'm compelled to look around the apartment just to make sure I'm still alone.

The door had been locked when I returned home just now, but that doesn't mean I'm completely safe. I grab the kitchen knife from the drawer, and then I run up to each window in the apartment to double-check it's locked. I then start checking the apartment for any hiding spots in case there's an intruder inside.

I stop when I see the top drawer in my bedroom slightly open. I freeze, I stare at it, and I refuse to blink.

My heart is thumping, and I can't get over the feeling of being watched. It makes me feel vulnerable, exposed, and I'm not supposed to feel like that in my own home.

Had I left the drawer open like that? It would have bothered me to see it like that, wouldn't it? I surely would have closed it in passing, just as I do with any drawer because it annoys me when it's left open.

I walk up to it, outstretch a hand forward, and contemplate whether to open it or not. I might not like what I'll find inside.

You're being ridiculous.

I grab the handle and push the drawer in. When I'm done checking every single place I think might serve as a hiding spot, I feel a lot better. I walk up to the windows and peek outside, searching for any figures that might be standing in the street below, silently watching me.

Nothing like that.

Then where did the ominous message come from?

I remember there are cameras in the building, so there's no way someone would have been able to get inside and leave this message without being noticed. There's a security office on the first floor. If I tell the guards employed there what happened, they can check the camera feed for me.

Good. Good.

I feel some of the control coming back to me. The feeling of being watched is dissipating, and so is the fear that has been clutching me for the past ten minutes. Strange how adrenaline can make sleepiness go away. I wouldn't be able to keep my eyes shut now even if I wanted to.

After taking one final look at the LEAVE THIS PLACE message, I fold the paper how I found it, slide it into my pocket, and exit the apartment. I call the elevator and wait impatiently for it to climb back up from the first floor.

The moment the door opens, I rush inside. I'm too slow to see someone standing inside and I bump into them hard.

"Whoa," Lee says as he braces me with his hands. "Where's the fire?"

"I'm so sorry, Lee. Didn't see you there," I blurt.

His face had been contorted into the amicable expression I'm used to. Seeing my distress, concern has etched itself on his face. "You okay?"

"Yeah, I just gotta head to the security office to get some stuff sorted."

"Why? What's up?"

I hadn't planned on telling Lee anything, so it must be my need for safety that takes over and starts talking.

"I found this in the mailbox," I say as I fish the paper out of my pocket.

The moment I say it, I feel so much better because I can see Lee listening intently. He wants to help me, I can see that even before he reads the message on the paper.

He unfolds the paper, gives me a dubious look, reads it, then frowns.

"What is this?" he asks.

"I found it in my mailbox just now," I repeat.

I bite my lip as I wait for Lee to analyze it, hoping against hope he has an answer to this mystery.

"Do you happen to know what it could be?"

***

Lee knows exactly what this is. He knows who sent it, too. Staring at the message, he fights against the urge to show his anger.

You're not going to ruin my plans.

"Yeah, I do know," he finally says with a soft smile that will hopefully lighten the situation.

"You do?" Andrea asks.

She doesn't look any less worried, but Lee likes that there's trust in her eyes. Trust, and a need to get behind Lee for protection.

Don't worry, my love. I'll keep you safe from the world. You're mine, and I'm going to protect you.

"Pranksters," Lee says as he crumbles up the paper.

He doesn't want Andrea looking at it anymore. He knows what type of person she is. The type to overthink things, to refuse to let them go until she has a definitive answer. If he gave her the paper back, she'd hang on to it, and only bad things could come from it.

"Pranksters?" Andrea asks.

"Yeah. There are some kids in the building that do these sorts of things from time to time," Lee says.

Andrea doesn't say anything for a little while. She seems to ponder Lee's explanation, perhaps trying to find logic in it.

"Wait, really?" she asks.

"Yeah. I should have warned you about them. They sometimes like to play pranks on new tenants. I'm really sorry for not telling you earlier. I honestly didn't think they'd do it again."

"Who exactly are they?"

"They live on one of the upper floors. Teens."

Andrea still doesn't look convinced, so Lee is already thinking of ways to convince her to let it go.

"Hey, it's just a harmless prank. It's stupid, but they're not hurting anyone."

"Yeah. This has happened before?"

"Yeah. A few times."

Andrea scratches her forehead. He lets out a sigh of relief. She suddenly looks a lot better, not as anxious as a few moments ago.

"So, you can forget all about it. If you react to it, they'll do it again. The best thing you can do is ignore it," Lee says.

Andrea nods. Lee flashes her a reassuring smile.

It doesn't work, because Andrea says, "I think I'll go have a look at security just in case."

Lee can't say anything to dissuade her from that. If he does, she might grow suspicious. He's thinking hard what to do next, how to stop Andrea from seeing the security video. If she sees it, she'll know Lee lied to her.

"I'll go with you," he finally says.

***

"I don't want to bother you with that," I say, even though I'm secretly thrilled Lee wants to accompany me.

"No bother at all. You're my tenant, and I want you to feel safe in the apartment," Lee says.

"I really appreciate it, Lee."

We step into the elevator and take it down to the first floor. Lee leads the way to the security office and knocks on the door. It takes a few minutes for the door to open and an elderly man with thick-rimmed glasses to poke his head out.

"Hi," Lee says. "We were wondering if we could check some of the camera footage."

The guard keeps staring at Lee incredulously, so I quickly add, "Someone's playing a prank on me, and I want to find out who it is."

The guard's head turns toward me when he hears my voice, he stares for a while, and then gives me a brusque nod.

"Okay." He opens the door for us.

"Thank you so much," I say.

The guard leads us inside. It's a small office, hardly bigger than a pantry, made to look even smaller because of the big monitor sitting on top of the desk.

"Here, knock yourselves out. I'm gonna go out for a smoke," the guard says.

"You're not gonna stay with us?" I ask.

"No. Why would I?"

"We might need your help to find the correct videos."

"Not my problem. You want to see it, you find it."

"What if we mess something up or cause damage to the office?"

The guard shrugs. "That's above my paygrade. I'm just here to look at the cameras from time to time."

It's clear that the guard doesn't care about the job. He's most likely already retired, and this is a side gig for him. Why should he bother to do more than the bare minimum?

"We'll take it from here, then," Lee says. "Enjoy your cigarette."

The guard takes the jacket off the hanger, puts it on, and steps outside without a word. At least he isn't giving us trouble about wanting to see the feed.

Lee sits at the chair and starts fiddling with the computer. He's clicking through things.

"You said you found it in your mailbox just now when you came home, right?" he asks.

"Yes." I cross my arms.

Lee double-clicks something and it opens the camera feed of the entrance of the building.

"It only has this one camera," he says.

"That should be good because it covers the main entrance. There's no way to get around that," I say.

"Yeah."

I watch as an unfamiliar tenant walks inside, opens her mailbox, and disappears out of view.

"This is from a week ago."

"Too old. I checked my mailbox the day before yesterday, and the message wasn't there."

"So whoever placed it there, did it either yesterday or today. Let me try and find it."

Lee clicks through some folders some more. This goes on for a few minutes. We don't talk. The only sounds in the room are the whirring of the computer and the clicking of the mouse.

"Cozy place, huh?" Lee breaks the silence after a while.

"Yeah. Very homey." I spin around to observe the office.

It's minimalistic. Not even a window. I don't think I'd be able to spend too long in here.

"Ah, shit," Lee says.

"What is it?" I turn toward him.

"There's a problem with the video recordings from this week."

"Oh, no. What kind of problems?"

Lee doesn't respond right away. He clicks some more for another minute or so and then says, "It looks like the files are corrupted."

"Corrupted?"

"Yeah. You'd be surprised how often this happens. Every third file here seems to be corrupted, though. I'm guessing they need to update their systems."

He tries a few more things to restore the files, but nothing works. Finally, he spins toward me in the chair and says, "I'm sorry, Andrea."

"It's not your fault," I say.

"Look, if it makes you feel better, those teens did the same thing to my previous tenant. I already spoke to the parents, because this kind of behavior is unacceptable. Actually, you know what? This sort of shit has to stop. I'm going to go talk to them again right now, give them a piece of my mind."

He gets up and brushes past me.

"Lee," I call out. "Lee, wait."

He opens the door and stops.

"It's fine. Forget about it," I say.

"No, Andrea. They need to know this isn't something to joke around with. What if you had called the police because of it? I'm going to talk to them."

"Lee, don't. Really, it's fine. I'm sure it won't happen again."

Lee looks like he's on the verge of agreeing, but a part of him still wants to go talk to those tenants.

"I already forgot about it. Okay?" I ask.

He slightly relaxes. Finally, he gives me a nod. "Fine. But if something like this happens again, I want to know right away, and I'm going to give them hell about it. Okay?"

"Yes."

"Good. Let's go back, then."

"And Lee? Thank you so much."

I want to hug him and kiss him for doing this with me and for being so protective. I bite down on that urge and give him a smile instead.

***

Lee smiles back. If Andrea decides to go back and check the security footage on her own, she's going to find this week's recordings missing, because Lee has deleted them while she wasn't looking.

No one is going to take Andrea away from him.

Chapter 15

Lately, I can't wake up properly. I sleep for eight hours, and I'm groggy for hours after waking up. Since moving into the new place almost two months ago, I've already slept in twice and missed two important meetings. My manager won't tolerate that much longer.

I chalk up the exhaustion to stress and the new environment I live in. I'm going to have to start going to bed earlier and improve my diet then, no big deal.

I haven't heard from Ryan ever since I blocked him (again), but I can't stop thinking about him. It's as if the dust has settled only recently, and now I'm suffering from the fallout.

It makes me sad sometimes because too many things remind me of my life with him. I can look at something that I never would have given a second glance in the past, and it'll remind me of a moment Ryan and I shared.

It'll pass in time, I keep telling myself. Meanwhile, I try to occupy myself as much as I can so I don't have time to think. A lot of that time is taken up by work, but outside of it? I still have time to think. I need some hobbies.

Before, I used to take Spanish lessons twice a week and I read a lot. Nowadays, I mostly waste time on my phone or watch Netflix. Having time to ourselves is important, yes, but I also firmly believe that we can't overindulge, otherwise we become too lazy and nothing makes us happy anymore.

I get my happiness from feeling accomplished. I want to get back into that. Maybe it's time to do so. Maybe that's the best way to get over Ryan.

It's Wednesday night. I'm done with work, and as much as I feel like taking a nap, I resist the urge. Instead, I sit down and start going through a list of things that I could adopt as my new hobby. The doorbell rings and, when I open the door, I see Lee standing in front of it with beers in his hand.

"Bad time?" he asks.

"No. Not at all. Come on in," I say.

I say it more on autopilot than anything else. I still don't think it's a good idea for me to be hanging out with my landlord, but, you know what? I enjoy Lee's company. Why shouldn't I at least indulge in finding new friends?

Or something more than that.

Lee walks in and places the beer cans on the coffee table in the living room. I can see his gaze drifting somewhere to the left, to the plain wall that has nothing on it.

I'm suddenly aware that the apartment might not be as clean as Lee expects it to be. He's my landlord, and this is his place, as much as I'd like to consider it my home.

"How's your mom?" I ask.

"Good. She's been a little better these days. It won't be long before she sinks back into those unbearable episodes of hers, but I'm just glad she's okay for now. We get to talk about things, and that's not something we do often lately."

I smile because there's nothing I can do to make him feel better. Telling him I'm sorry is something he must have heard a million times by now, and I know I'd hate to hear it over and over. Sorry is a word that doesn't make anyone feel better. It's just a formality we use to show compassion that society wants us to show.

"Please, have a seat. It's your place, after all," I say.

"No, no. While you're renting, this is *your* place, and I'm just a guest here," Lee says when he sits.

I appreciate that he's helping me feel so at home. I know that the places we rent are never ours, but we tend to get cocooned inside them and consider them our homes. I have to admit that I've already taken a liking to this place.

For the first week or so, I considered it a place where I spend the night, not home. I guess I was afraid of getting used to it like I did in Ryan's place and then having to leave. But now that some time has passed, I've started decorating the apartment with my own things.

In fact, I don't see myself leaving any time soon, unless Lee decides he doesn't want me here anymore.

"So, everything okay with the place?" Lee asks. "No other plumbing problems, AC problems, or anything like that?"

"Everything's fine. Thanks again for being on top of that all the time."

I take a seat next to him.

"Here." He offers me a can.

It's been a while since I imbibed, and beer is not really my thing.

"Actually, I'm more in the mood for some wine," I say. "I got a bottle in the fridge. Want to share it?"

Lee nods. "Sure."

Twenty minutes later, we're on our second glass of wine and a lot more open to each other. There's no awkward tension between us. The ice has been broken, and we're talking, joking, laughing.

"Say, I never asked you. What do you do for a living?" I ask.

"I'm an architect," Lee says.

I sit upright. "Really?"

"Mhm," he says as he takes a sip of wine.

"Were you the one who designed this building?"

Lee throws his head back and laughs. "No. I designed a building in Chicago, two in New York, and one in a small town in Ohio."

"That's so interesting."

I'm leaning my head against the palm of my hand as I listen to Lee. I want to know more about his work because I've never met someone with such an interesting occupation. I have so many questions on my mind—like, how did he become an architect, why, what his vision is, etc.

"It's just a boring job like any other. Most days, I design blueprints or have meetings with engineers," Lee says.

"You're being humble," I say. "I want to know more about it. Did you always want to be an architect?"

"The idea came to me when I was in high school. I always liked building and putting things together, so I figured I might as well go to a college that would let me do that."

"It must be a dream come true to do something you love," I say as I take a sip.

"Well, it's okay. It's not like I can build whatever I like. My desires for architecture are slightly... different."

"Oh yeah? What kinds of things would you like to build? Secret dungeons used for perverse things?"

I wouldn't normally ask something like that, but I'm a little tipsy, and it's helping me be myself a little more than I usually would.

Lee leans back, looks at me, and says, "Apartments with secret passages that would allow me to spy on its residents."

There's dead silence between us.

Then, I burst into laughter.

"You almost had me there," I say.

He shrugs with a chuckle and takes a sip of wine. His glass is empty, so he refills it and adds some more to mine.

My mind is still stuck on the mystery of the building visions that Lee has. He hasn't given me a straight answer, which means he's probably either embarrassed to share it or wants to keep it a secret for some other reason.

Usually, people hide things behind humor. They think they're really clever about it, but the only thing they're doing is revealing that they're hiding something. And the more they hide it, the more glaringly obvious it becomes.

So, what is Lee hiding? Maybe I'm just overthinking it. Maybe he's the kind of person that likes to keep his head down and keep working, let the results speak for themselves.

"I'm surprised you're single, Lee. I thought women were all over architects," I say.

It's definitely the wine talking instead of me. The moment I say that, heat rushes to my face. I feel exhilarated at what I just said because it's like I'm dancing on the edge of something very new, very dangerous, but also very arousing.

Lee looks embarrassed. "Well, I guess I don't go out often enough."

More silence sits between us before Lee clears his throat and asks, "What about you? You said you lived with your boyfriend before this, right? How do you like single life?"

"I've just been taking time to adjust, you know? It was a big change for me."

"I can't imagine. Can I ask what happened between the two of you? I'm sorry, I don't mean to overstep any boundaries."

"No, it's fine. Things sort of just changed between us. We weren't as close as before, and we spent less and less time with each other, and that led to us growing even more distant. I guess we just changed in different ways. I think I stopped loving him a long time ago but stayed with him because it was the only thing I knew."

"I'm guessing you two tried to work things out," Lee says.

"Yeah, but it was already too late by then. Ryan wanted us to continue trying to fix us, but I wanted out. So, I left him."

"That must have been tough."

"Making that decision was easy. Sticking to it was the hard part."

"But you stuck to it?"

"Yes." *For now.* "He wanted to see me, but I blocked him everywhere."

"It's for the best." Lee nods. "Nothing good can come out of meeting with an ex. Believe me, I know."

We stare at each other for a long moment. Lee leans toward me, and I do nothing to stop him. The voice that screams he is my landlord is merely a whisper. I'm no longer on the border with that dangerous, arousing feeling. I'm well into its territory, and I see no way to go back.

Instead, when our lips meet, I instinctively return the kiss. It feels…

Nothing like I expect it to because, the moment I kiss him, my mind conjures up the image of Ryan. I recoil as if burned, realizing what I've just done.

Lee looks confused. I messed up so badly. The relaxation given to me by the wine is gone, replaced by sudden tension. Since moving here, I've had fantasies about Lee. This kiss has given me a bitter taste of reality and I now understand I've been fooling myself.

All this time, I was imagining a scenario in my head that's far from reality. I'm very attracted to Lee, yes, but he and I would never work as a couple. It's one of those things that I simply can't explain. The chemistry between us was strong, and it's as if the actual contact dissolved it.

The best way I can explain it is like meeting someone in person you've been chatting with online for a long time and realizing the two are completely different worlds.

When I look at Lee now, I don't see a potential dating partner. I see my landlord. I see a man who could have given me comfort in my difficult time after breaking up with Ryan. He's so much more than that, just not for me.

I hop to my feet and say, "I'm sorry, Lee. I don't know what I was thinking."

He stands. "Hey, it's all right."

"No, it's not. I'm sorry, there's just so much on my mind these days. And I'm still thinking about…"

"About your boyfriend," Lee finishes the sentence. "I understand. Hey, it's okay. If you want to take things slow, we can take them slow."

But slow isn't the pace I want to take. I want to stop entirely.

"I'm sorry, I'm feeling really lightheaded all of a sudden. I think I'm going to lie down for a bit," I say.

If that's not a clear enough sign for Lee to leave, I'll have to become more direct, and I hate doing that.

"Oh, absolutely. I'll see myself out," he says.

"Thank you." I give him a friendly smile.

I keep my distance from him as he goes out the door because I don't want to give him any signs he might misread.

This is all my fault. This kiss never would have happened if I'd set the boundaries right away. I really don't want to move out of this apartment, but I also don't know how I'm going to look Lee in the eyes after this.

If enough time passes, things might go back to normal. Please, God, let them go back to normal.

"Hey, thanks for inviting me in," Lee says.

"Sure. I had fun," I say.

He stands there a moment longer as if expecting something. When I do nothing about it, he smiles and says, "Okay. Well, you have a good rest, Andrea."

The moment I close the door, I allow myself to breathe a heavy sigh. I feel as though I've just run a marathon.

For the next ten minutes, I pace the living room up and down, considering the implications of my actions. Is Lee going to force me out of the apartment? No, he can't do it based on this, right?

No, but he can evict me if he deems me a bad tenant. He wouldn't do that, though, would he? No, Lee is a nice guy. He understands I'm going through a tough breakup right now.

I calm myself down. The next time I see him, I'll apologize.

I'm sure he's going to understand.

***

Lee barges into his apartment. He wants to slam the door shut, but he can't because Andrea might hear him having a fit. He closes it, locks it, and walks into the living room.

The old snake of his mother is sitting in her wheelchair, watching TV. The noise coming from it makes Lee even angrier.

He picks up a plant pot and chucks it at the screen. The flatscreen cracks, hits the back of the shelf, and then topples forward onto the floor. The noises coming from the TV stop entirely.

Lee's mother looks at him with startlement and fear. It gives him satisfaction to know she's afraid of him.

Even before she opens her mouth, he says, "Not a word, you old bitch! This is all your fault!"

He needs a scapegoat right now, even if it's someone as innocent as his mother. No, she's not innocent. The stupid bitch has been trying to meddle in his life ever since Andrea moved here, and even before that.

Her words must have planted a worm of doubt into his mind, and it ruined his chances with Andrea. He was so close to making her his—really his. He probably won't get another chance.

No, it still isn't too late. Andrea just needs time to think things through. She likes Lee, he's sure of it. Why else would she invite him over for food, for drinks, and kiss him? She likes him. He just needs to be patient and bide his time in order to claim her for himself.

Here's the plan: He's going to continue being friendly to her. He'll pretend he's not interested in her romantically. That's going to spark her interest again. Women are like that. The more you push them away, the more they want you. The more you show interest, the more repulsed they are.

He's going to be friendly to her, hang out with her from time to time. And then when the time is right, he's going to kiss her again. And this time, she's going to keep going. She's going to let him take her, and they are going to be happy together.

"The TV," a small, timid voice next to him says.

Lee has been pacing the room for a few minutes now without realizing it. When his mother grabs his attention, he goes from somewhat composed to angry again.

"You need a time-out!" he says as he begins rolling her toward the closet.

His mother lets out an animalistic whimper, but no perceptible words come out of her mouth. She wails as he rolls her into the closet. Lee ignores her as he shuts her inside. She can sleep in there tonight.

It's going to be painful on her old bones, but it serves her right for pissing him off.

As for Andrea…

Lee's going to pay her a visit tonight. She gave him a taste of something he desperately yearned for, only to yank it away. He wants more, and he's going to get it.

And this time, he isn't going to be as gentle with her because she, too, has made him angry.

Chapter 16

I wake up to my phone blaring loudly on my nightstand.

It doesn't startle me like it usually does. Rather, it seems to grow louder and louder, and somewhere along the line, I realize it isn't a sound in my dream but my alarm.

"Ugh." The sound escapes my mouth as I reach for the nightstand.

When I look at the screen, I'm suddenly wide awake.

It's not the alarm at all. It's my manager, Dwight.

"Oh, shit," I say, my voice still toad-like from just waking up.

I jump into a sitting position, clear my throat a few times, and then answer the phone. I don't even have time to think about how to greet Dwight. I can already tell how pissed he is from the incessant ringing.

"Hell—"

"Andrea, where in the goddamn hell are you?!"

His screaming into the phone makes my ear hurt.

"I'm sorry, I know I'm late!" I shoot up to my feet. "I don't know what's going on. I set three alarms and somehow slept through them. I think I'm gonna have to go to a doctor to see why I'm so tired all the time."

"Well, do it later because that super important client is here, and I'm frigging tired of making excuses for you! Do you realize how unprofessional this looks?"

"I'm sorry! I'm on my way! I'll be there in twenty minutes!"

I'm already putting on my socks and hopping into my jeans.

"Hurry it up!" Dwight says and then hangs up.

My head feels like it weighs a ton. My eyelids want to close, and I have to splash water on my face to sober up. I should be feeling wide awake after such an insane wake-up call, but I feel like I could go to bed and sleep another six hours.

Seriously, what the hell is going on with me?

I wash my face and stop when I notice something in the mirror. I crane my head and look at the bruise on the side of my neck. It's thumb-sized, and I wonder how I got it. I don't remember hitting myself anywhere, and I think I'd remember hurting my neck.

Not only that, but my entire body feels sort of... sore, as if I had a sports massage and now my muscles are all tender to the touch.

I need to get a grip. This is, like, the fifth time that I've slept in, in two months. Something's definitely wrong with me. I'm either overworked, or I have a condition I don't know about that's making me feel tired like this.

On my way out of the apartment, I happen to glance at the lonesome wall that has no decorations on it, and I see something that wasn't there before.

A handprint.

I walk up to the wall and inspect the smudge on it just to make sure I'm seeing it right. Damn, it really is a handprint.

At this point, I'm feeling slightly unnerved. Paranoid, even. I look around myself just to make sure I'm not being watched.

I suddenly remember the LEAVE THIS PLACE note I found in the mailbox. Jesus, what if I'm not paranoid? What if something really is wrong with this place?

No, that's nonsense. I'm just under too much stress and it's causing me to jump at shadows, that's all.

Living alone, the only conclusion I could reach about the handprint is the fact that I left it there. There's nothing else that could have happened.

The problem is I don't ever get close to that wall and definitely not so close as to leave a handprint. I know that for sure because I'm very careful about dirtying the walls, especially a blank one that would have stains visible right away.

I reach forward to compare the handprint on the wall to mine, my heart pumping vigorously in my chest. I inch closer, and closer, and then…

A loud ding in the room startles me.

"Jesus," I say as I reach into my pocket and pull my phone out.

A message from Dwight urging me to hurry up snaps my attention away from the wall. I leave the apartment, forgetting about the mysterious handprint for the moment.

A sense of déjà vu overcomes me as I sit on the train, waiting to reach my destination. This time, I worry more, because I know that even if the meeting with the client goes okay, Dwight is going to give me an earful. I'm partly hoping the ride on the subway doesn't come to an end.

When I finally arrive at work, Dwight is standing in front of the reception, tapping his foot on the floor. It feels like the millionth time that he's doing that.

"I'm sorry, Dwight! I'm really sorry! I'll get to—"

"I don't wanna hear it, Andrea!" Dwight shouts loud enough to cause heads to turn. "This isn't college where you can skip classes as you like! If this happens one more time, you're fired!"

Without allowing me a word in, he spins around and stomps out of the room, leaving me alone with all the curious eyes of my coworkers plastered to me.

Okay, now I definitely need to see a doctor, and as soon as I'm done with work because my job is at stake.

The meeting with the client goes okay despite me being late and them being annoyed. Afterward, I focus on finishing the reports I've been working on. It's one of those days where a minute feels like an hour.

I'm really starting to worry about my health because I've never felt like this before. Maybe it's something insignificant like iron deficiency, but what if it's serious, like diabetes? What if it's cancer? I really, really hope it's nothing that serious.

As soon as I finish all the meetings for the day, I schedule an appointment with my GP. I'm lucky because they have an available slot later this afternoon.

I head there right after work. This morning, the only thing I cared about was getting confirmation that something is indeed wrong with me so I can show the notice to Dwight. Right now, I don't care about my stupid manager or the company. I just want to make sure I'm okay.

While I sit in the waiting room, I once again think about what it could possibly be. It's something, I know for sure. I'm not the kind of person who sleeps in. Maybe I really am just overworked? Or maybe I'm getting too old?

Maybe it's the stress I've pushed under the rug.

Funny, but I don't feel stressed. Is that true, though?

The entire move and breakup were stressful enough. Just because I don't feel like it's impacting me mentally doesn't mean it's not taking a toll on my body. Then there's also the whole thing with Lee that happened yesterday.

Shit. Lee.

I only just then remember that we kissed yesterday, and that causes another bout of panic to bloom inside me.

Okay, so maybe I *am* stressed. Either way, the doctor will be able to tell me what's wrong and hopefully give me a solution because I don't know what to do anymore. I've started going to bed earlier, so getting enough sleep is not it. I could improve my diet, sure, but how much could a diet actually impact my ability to wake up?

You know what? I'm worrying myself even more than I should, so I'll just wait until I'm inside the doctor's office to see what's wrong.

As I continue waiting, I once again become aware of the painful bruise on my neck. How did it get there? Something really weird is going on. I can't tell what, but I suddenly get this urge to take extra precautions. I think I might install a camera to see what I'm doing in the middle of the night.

Who knows, maybe I'm sleepwalking and hurting myself in the process. That would explain the handprint on the wall. There's no other conclusion to reach. I live on the fourth floor, and if I'm sleepwalking, I need to know about it as soon as possible because I don't want to do something crazy like jump out the window or whatever.

The time I spend in the waiting room is killing me. I keep glancing at my watch, hoping for the nurse to call my name.

Relief washes over me when she finally does. I practically jump as I enter the office. After a series of questions, the doctor comes in and asks me the same questions.

I explain to him what's wrong, and he runs some tests. He asks me if I'm taking any drugs, to which I say no. It's true. I've never even smoked weed, let alone anything stronger. Hell, I even try to stay away from painkillers as much as I can.

The doctor dismisses the possibility of various conditions like cancer—much to my relief—and tells the nurse to draw my blood. He says the results will be ready in a few days when I come back for a check-up.

He tells me to take a few days off work in the meantime, if possible, and rest. I tell him I'm already doing what I can to reduce my workload and sleep enough, but he doesn't look convinced.

"The bloodwork will tell us what's really wrong. If you have a deficiency, we'll know what to do," he says.

I'm not happy that I didn't get any concrete answers, but I'm hopeful about the bloodwork.

On my way home, I'm instinctively touching the bruise on my neck. It's more tender to the touch than it was this morning. Looks darker, too.

What happened there?

That reminds me that I need to solve my sleepwalking problem if it's there. Who knows? Maybe it's not sleepwalking at all, and I'm just hitting myself in my sleep or something. It's not unheard of that people flail their arms in their sleep.

I stop by an electronics shop and buy a night-vision camera. I don't need anything fancy, just a camera to detect whether I'm doing something that I shouldn't.

When I return home, I drop my purse on the counter and reach inside to find the camera. I grasp it just in time when the doorbell rings.

It's Lee.

I've been dreading our encounter ever since last night, but it was inevitable. I guess it's best to get this over with as soon as possible. I let go of the camera in my purse and head to the door.

"Hey," he says, but there's less enthusiasm in his voice than usual.

"Hi, Lee. What's up?" I ask.

I don't want him to come inside. Not right now. That's why I asked him *what's up* in an attempt to make it clear I'm open only to brief communication.

Lee puts his hands into his pockets. His shoulders are tense, and I can tell he's not happy about having this talk, either.

"I know you probably just got off work, and I don't want to bother you. I was hoping we could talk if you have a minute," he says.

Usually, these one-minute talks end up being a lot longer than that. Still, I can either have the unpleasant conversation now, or I can postpone it and have it later when it's going to be equally unpleasant. If I don't do it now, though, I'll keep stressing over it, and I don't think I can afford any more stress on top of what I already have on my plate.

"Yeah, sure," I say. "I have a couple of minutes."

I step aside to let him in.

"Thanks," he says.

He stops in the middle of the living room. His eyes fall on the wall where I found the handprint this morning. I don't know if he sees it and chooses not to mention it or he's too nerve-wracked to see it.

"So, about last night," he starts. "I want to say I'm sorry. I know you have a lot on your mind right now, and I probably shouldn't have done what I did. Wine doesn't affect me well, I guess."

He tries to crack a smile at that last sentence, but it trails into a rictus.

"No, it's fine. You're right, I do have a lot going on right now and I'm not ready for… well, any additional changes in my life. And I really don't want to complicate our landlord-tenant relationship."

Lee nods. "Yep. I totally understand. And I agree."

***

But Lee doesn't agree. He's forcing himself to smile, but inside, he feels like he's melting. Andrea is slipping away, and the more he tries to reach her, the farther she seems to grow distant.

And he was so close. So close.

His eyes drift to the handprint on the wall, the one he left last night on his way out of Andrea's apartment after sexually abusing her.

He was rough with her yesterday. He hadn't planned on being that way, but once he started having sex with her, all the bottled-up anger came bursting out. He called her all sorts of names, slapped her, choked her and, when he was done using her, he quietly exited the apartment.

She has a bruise on her neck. Seeing his mark on her arouses Lee. It's bittersweet, though. He left his mark on her like she's his property, but she isn't really his. Not always, anyway.

Only when night falls and when she is deeply asleep and unable to say no. During the day, a thick wall separates them. Lee hates that because he wants to touch her, hold her, be close to her, and she won't let him.

"I'm really glad we could come to that understanding," Andrea says.

She looks a lot more relaxed now that she feels like the worst is behind her.

"Absolutely," Lee says. "But I'm not just your landlord. I'm your friend, too. If you ever need someone to talk to, I'll be here for you."

Because I love you, the words are poised on his lips, but he doesn't speak them.

Andrea smiles. He can tell she's dismissive of his suggestion. That kiss last night changed everything. Lee now realizes it's all his fault for rushing. He should have waited with the kiss, but he had been so afraid of losing her that he allowed his urge to get the better of him.

It's still not too late, though. If he continues hanging out with her, she might start liking him again. She would see he's the perfect guy for her. He would always treat her right and never hurt her. Not like her ex-boyfriend Ryan.

***

I'm glad the conversation went so smoothly. At least, I think it went smoothly. Lee seems perfectly understanding, but behind that smile and those eyes, I think I detect something hidden. Is it disappointment because nothing more came of our kiss?

It's all my fault, and I want to apologize to Lee, but I feel like doing so will only loop us back into the conversation about the kiss, and I really don't want to get back to that.

"Thanks again, Lee. I'm glad we got that out of the way," I say and go back to digging through my purse.

I locate the camera again, and I'm about to pull it out when Lee says, "Yeah. Well, I won't hold you up any longer. Should probably check on my mother, anyway."

The camera slips from my fingers and falls back into the endless pit inside the purse. I give up on it for now and see Lee out.

He's standing in front, that familiar, expectant look on his face. I can't tell what he wants from me. Is there anything that hasn't been said yet? Does he have anything on his mind he wants to share?

"You have a great day, Andrea," he says with a smile.

He turns and leaves, his hands in his pockets, his shoulders tense. His gait is stiff and mechanical, and his gaze is plastered to the floor. I ignore it as I shut the door and lock the apartment.

I let out an exasperated sigh and run my hand through my hair. Okay. I'm glad that's done.

Returning to my purse on the counter, I finally pull out the camera, open the box, and read the instructions on how to set it up. There's way too much text for me to handle on the manual right now, so I give up on it.

I'm going to set it up as soon as I'm feeling a little better.

Chapter 17

I went to bed earlier the previous night, so it's easier for me to get up this morning. I feel lightweight as I get up and get ready for work. I open the mailbox and see the bills inside. I reach for them until I remember I don't want to lug those things with me all day long, so I leave them there instead. I commute to work and begin doing paperwork. I only need one coffee to kickstart me this morning, too.

The day goes by without a hitch. No meetings I'm late to. No angry clients. No problems from Dwight. When I'm done for the day, I pack up and go back home. By then, I'm feeling sleepy again. Probably accumulated exhaustion.

I enter the building, open the mailbox to grab the bills, and—

Oh God. Please, no. Not again.

I see it sitting inside the mailbox. The familiar little slip of paper nestled on top of the envelopes.

For the longest moment, I don't move. I consider not taking it. If I close the mailbox and pretend I never saw it, or even better, if I just throw it away, it'll be like it never existed in the first place, right?

Of course not. Wishful thinking.

Hoping against hope that it's not what I think it is, I take the paper out. It takes me some extra time to brace myself to unfold it. When I do, my heart sinks.

PLEASE LEAVE, the message says this time.

Without thinking, I crumple the paper and throw it in the trash can. I rush to the elevator and slam the button to call it. It's on the ninth floor, of course.

Why am I so worried about the message? It's just pranksters. Lee has said so himself. Just teenagers playing around.

Something about the whole thing refuses to let me calm down. Something is off about the entire situation.

The elevator has made it to the sixth floor, but I don't wait for it. I spin on my heel and walk to the security office. After rapping on the door for what feels like a whole minute, I hear the knob turning.

The same, old security guard from last time pokes his head out. "Yes?"

"I need to see the security footage," I say. The guard hesitates, so I sternly add, "Now."

He opens the door, lets me in, and steps outside without a word. I have no idea how to access the security feed, so I begin by going through the folders. All of the files are marked with numbers, which I realize soon are dates.

I need the one from today. It had to have happened today because the paper wasn't there this morning. Whoever put it there did so while I was at work. I swear to God, if it's those damn kids that Lee has warned me about, I'm going to find out who they are and give their parents an earful.

After a few minutes of searching, I see the video I'm looking for. I double-click it and hope it isn't corrupted like last time. It opens without an issue. It shows the entrance at night. It displays the time as midnight.

I fast forward to a little after 8 a.m., which is when I see myself opening the mailbox and leaving for work. I speed up the video and watch as people walk in and out as time passes. No one even glances at the mailbox. And then, I see a woman walk in. Before I can slow the video down, I see her approaching the mailbox, slipping something inside, and leaving the building.

I rewind, slow the video down, and watch again.

She's around my age, I think. The video quality is not high enough for me to tell. Her shoulders are tense, and she's looking around, as if pursued by someone. She approaches the mailbox, rummages through her purse, and pulls out a little piece of paper. She slides it into my mailbox, looks left and right, and then hurries out of the building.

I replay the video. I'm trying to find any discernible features on the woman. Anything that would tell me who she is. More importantly, I'm hit with something unpleasant as I realize that Lee was wrong.

It wasn't teenagers. It was a woman.

But why? Why would she do that? For the first time since moving here, something unpleasant coils inside my gut. Something akin to fear.

Am I in danger?

The video is too long, so I quickly snip the part with the woman in the frame and save it like that. I open the internet browser and email the video to myself and to Becca. I need to study it in order to find out who this person is and what she wants.

I rush out of the security office, take the elevator to my apartment, and I call Becca. She picks up on the first ring. "Hello?"

"Becca, listen. I need your help. I sent a video to your email. I need you to help me figure out who the person in the video is."

"Uh, what?"

"I'll explain everything, but I really need your help right now. Watch the video and we'll talk after that."

"Okay…"

Becca sounds confused when we hang up, and rightly so. I pace around my apartment for a few minutes like a caged lion before my phone starts ringing. It's Becca.

"Yes?" I answer.

"Okay, so I watched your video, and I'm even more confused. Who the hell is that woman?" Becca asks.

"That's what I need your help finding out."

I explain everything to her, starting with how I found the message in my mailbox a while ago, dismissed it, and then found it again this morning.

"What do you think she wants?" Becca asks.

"I don't know. That's what I'm worried about."

"Do you think it might be an angry client from your company?"

"No. I would have recognized her. And I haven't crossed anybody like that."

There's a pause on the line before Becca speaks up again. "Andrea, do you think you might be in danger?"

I hesitate before answering. "I don't know. That's why I want to find out who she is."

"Yeah. Listen, there's something I need to tell you."

The tone at which she says that tells me it's gonna be bad news. I swallow and wait for her to continue.

Becca clears her throat. "Jacob and I think there's something wrong with your place."

It's a short sentence, a vague one, but it's enough to send an icy bullet straight down my spine.

"What do you mean by that?" I ask. "What are you not telling me?"

"I don't know, Andrea. Something just felt off about your apartment."

"Off how?"

"Look, I can't explain it. I just… I don't know. I just didn't like it. I felt… Never mind."

"No, tell me."

I'm getting frustrated with Becca. You can't just drop a bomb like that one on someone and then say never mind. I need to know what she thinks is wrong with my apartment so I can take the necessary precautions to protect myself.

"You know what? It's probably just my imagination anyway," Becca says.

"Becs. There's a woman that keeps dropping messages in my mailbox telling me to leave. Whatever you think is wrong, I need you to not keep me in the dark.

Becca sighs. "That night when Jacob and I visited you, I felt like we weren't alone there."

I didn't think a chill could run down my spine again with the same intensity, but it does.

"Oh?" I ask, barely a ghost of a word. "Why did you think that?"

"That's the thing. I don't know. I just felt paranoid."

"Well, there's gotta be a concrete reason. Something that made you feel that way."

"Maybe just an accumulation of things. The fact that the apartment is so spacious, which, to me, is already scary enough. And then there's the whole low rent and friendly landlord thing. For him to just show up like that… Like, the timing seemed too perfect."

The chill is gone. I'd hate to say it, but Becca has lost me. I now understand her suspicions are in the wrong place.

"I understand why you'd be so skeptical, Becs," I say. "I was, too. But do you think I didn't do my research before moving here?"

"So then, what's with the mystery woman and the threatening messages?"

"They're not threatening," I say, realizing I'm focused on the wrong thing.

"You get what I'm trying to say."

I can envision Becca rolling her eyes.

"That's a completely separate thing. But I need to get to the bottom of it. That's why I need your help. Please, Becca.

I haven't lived alone in a long time. Do you know how scary this is? I can't rely on a boyfriend to protect me in case I have a stalker problem."

"I'll help you. You don't even need to ask me. I know a guy, but I'm not sure how long it'll take him to analyze the video."

"You actually know someone who can help with it?"

"Yeah, some digital marketing guy."

I have no idea how a digital marketing guy can help in a situation like this one, but I'm too desperate to prod for details. Right now, I just want to trust that Becca is going to help me out.

"I'll take it," I say.

"Okay. I'll call you in a few days, as soon as he figures something out. Okay?"

"Yeah. Thanks, Becca."

"And Andrea?"

"Yes?"

"Please be careful. Always be aware of your surroundings, especially now. Ask your landlord for help if you have to."

That's right, I haven't even told her about kissing Lee yet. That's going to have to wait until next time because I really don't feel like talking about it right now.

"I will," I simply say before we hang up.

Left alone in silence, I go to the bedroom and watch the video of the woman on my phone over and over. I try to zoom in, take note of her facial features, but it's no use. Even if I somehow got a clear look at her, it wouldn't mean anything, because I would have no way of locating her.

I give up on the video for now, deciding that it's more destructive for me than it is helpful. I need to take my mind off things, and I conveniently remember that I still haven't set up the camera for my night recording.

Following the manual keeps me occupied, and by the time I set up the camera, I've calmed down significantly. I start to think that maybe all this isn't as big a deal as I initially thought. So far, the mysterious woman has left two messages for me telling me to leave, but nothing more than that.

Does she know there's a camera in the building? She must, just as she knows the passcode to the entrance. It's the only way she could have entered, unless someone let her in via the intercom.

The question still remains: Who is she and why is she doing what she's doing?

To be safe, I'm going to keep the front door locked at all times. I'm also going to buy pepper spray. Better safe than sorry.

Chapter 18

The very next morning, I get out of a meeting to see a missed call from Becca. I take my break right away and call her back.

"Becca?" I ask.

"Listen, I got something," Becca says.

"What is it?"

"The woman you're looking for is Helena Myers."

I'm dumbstruck. Becca already has a full name on her?

"I'm going to send you all the info on her shortly," she says.

"How the hell did you find that out so fast?"

"The guy I know is *really* good. He noticed the subway logo on her jacket and looked up all the female employees working in the city. From there, it was pretty easy finding a match."

Wow. I don't have the words to express my surprise. I hadn't expected Becca to come up with anything for at least a few days. This is moving just a little too fast for my taste.

"So, are you gonna go talk to her?" Becca asks.

"You even have an address?" I ask.

"Yeah. What good would all of this be without an address?"

"Yeah. I'm going to talk to her."

"Want me to come with you?"

I consider that for a moment. I would love to have Becca come with me, but no. I need to do this alone. This is my problem, and I feel like bringing someone along would only make the woman—Helena Myers—clam up and become defensive even more.

"No, I'm good. I'll go pay her a visit right after work. Listen, thanks a lot for doing this for me. I owe you."

"Just be careful, please."

"I will."

I spend the next fifteen minutes going through Helena Myers's social media. There's not much to see since the profiles are locked, but her LinkedIn shows she's an engineer employed at the city's subway. That at least tells me she's of a somewhat sound mind and not a junkie that can't be reasoned with.

Her address shows she lives in an apartment in a peaceful neighborhood on the other side of the city.

I can hardly focus on work because I'm already conjuring up a dialogue in my head. What am I going to tell Helena? How do I approach her and not have her slam the door in my face? What's the first thing I should tell her?

Hi, Helena. Glad to finally meet you. No, too snide.

You already know who I am, don't you? No, too threatening.

Hi. I just want to talk, that's all. No, too timid.

As worktime approaches its end, I become more and more anxious. I vacillate from angry at Helena to afraid of how she's going to react to me showing up at her doorstep. Those emotions disappear the moment I board the train to Helena's address.

I get a message from Becca wishing me luck and I thank her. Helena's street is quiet. I climb the steps to her building, contemplating how I'm going to get her to open the door for me. Luckily, someone is exiting the building just then and they hold the door open for me. I thank them with a smile and slip inside.

Helena lives on the fifth floor, which I take the elevator to. When I'm in front of her door, I take a moment to mentally prepare myself. Then, I ring the doorbell and wait.

I see a shadow move across the peephole and I'm aware that Helena is watching me. For a moment, I think she's going to retreat and pretend she isn't home, and I'm already prepared to shout I know she's in there.

Instead, I hear the lock clicking and the door suddenly opens. In front of me is the woman herself.

She's a lot prettier than in the pixelated video I saw. One look at her is enough for me to determine she's a little erratic. Something about her wide stare and tense body radiates that.

We stare at each other in silence. I'm the one who speaks up first.

"Hi, Helena. I assume you know who I am."

The words come smoothly out of my mouth.

"How did you find me?" Helena asks.

Her voice is on the deeper end, but it sounds sensual, like a narrator of bedtime stories. At the same time, there's a quiver in there.

I want to skip all the details of how I figured out who she is and where she lives, so I say, "Can we please talk?"

Helena stiffens her lips. She shifts her weight from one foot to the other, and then opens the door wider for me to get in.

"Thank you," I say.

Her apartment is smaller than mine, but it's cute as heck. The pink colors, the scented candles, and the flowers belie Helena's stern attitude. She ushers me into the living room and gestures to the couch. I thank her as I sit. She sits opposite of me and crosses her legs.

"I guess you know why I'm here," I say. "And I reckon you didn't leave me those messages because you thought it would be a funny prank."

"No, I didn't," she says.

I lean on my knees. "Who are you, and why did you do it?"

Helena licks her lips and uncrosses her legs. "I'm gonna get some water. You want something to drink?"

"I'm good, thanks."

She gets up and walks out of the room. In a bit, she's back with two glasses of water with ice.

"In case you get thirsty," she says as she puts the glasses on the table.

"Thanks," I say.

She settles on the sofa, crosses her legs again, and says, "I lived in that apartment before you."

It comes as a surprise to me. All this time, I haven't considered the possibility once that Helena Myers was a tenant in the same apartment where I live.

"Really?" I ask.

"Yes. Only for a month, though."

Something bad happened to her while she lived there, I can tell. She doesn't need to tell me so I would know. There's a hint of warning to her tone that I'm just barely able to discern.

Just like the messages. They weren't a threat. They were a warning.

"Did something happen to you?" I ask.

"Yes. Something did happen. But I don't think you'll believe me."

My assumption about Helena had been right. She's very erratic. She always does something with her hands and legs—never a moment where she's sitting still.

"Well, I'm here now, and you left those messages to me because you obviously think I'm in some sort of danger. That's why you want me to leave, right?"

"Yes."

"So, what is it?"

Helena swallows. She stares at me for a moment, maybe trying to read my face to determine whether I'm going to believe her or not. In the end, it doesn't matter because she takes the plunge.

"That apartment is haunted," she says.

"Haunted?" I ask.

"Yes. I know it sounds crazy, but just hear me out. At night, I would hear footsteps in my living room. I'd go out there to check it out and no one was there. I would find handprints on walls. I'd have trouble waking up, and when I woke up, I'd find new bruises on my body."

In the first half of her explanation, I wasn't buying it, but when she mentions bruises and trouble waking up, cold sweat breaks out on my skin.

"Bruises?" I ask. "Where?"

"Everywhere. My neck, my chest, my arms, legs. And whenever I woke up, I'd feel so heavy. It's like the apartment was draining my energy."

I'm hung up on the bruises and difficulty waking up. I'm not really listening to the haunted part.

"You don't believe me," she says.

"No, I do. I mean, I have trouble waking up, too. And I woke up bruised recently, too. But…"

"But you don't believe it's haunted."

I consider what to say next. "I think there's probably a logical explanation for it."

"Like what?"

"I don't know. Maybe the bed is too hard and we don't even feel ourselves getting bruised. And maybe we have trouble waking up because, I don't know. There has to be an explanation."

"What about footsteps? What about my things that kept disappearing? What about the handprints and fingerprints on various surfaces?"

I don't answer.

Helena leans forward. "Look, I don't care if you're a believer or not. I'm just telling you what I experienced. Sometimes at night, I would dream about certain things. Someone whispering into my ear, touching me, and I would open my eyes to see a dark figure retreating out of view. I would be too sleepy to get up and I'd fall asleep immediately after that, but I would see it. I'm telling you, something is wrong with that place."

I consider it all. I'm not entirely opposed to the idea that a place could be haunted, I just don't believe those things manifest so aggressively. Like, there might be a hint of it, but nothing as direct as Helena described it. This isn't a movie.

Still, a lot of the things she mentioned are a little too similar to my experience, and that's unnerving. The question is, is it the apartment, or is it all in our heads?

"I'll admit it's really weird," I say.

"But you don't believe me," Helena says.

"Do I think the apartment is haunted? No, I don't think so. But I do think there's something wrong with it. Maybe black mold, or something inside the apartment impacting our health. I'm going to talk to Lee and have it investigated."

Helena leans back. "Don't bother. I already tried talking to him while I lived there. He always says he'll help, but he never does anything about it."

"I'm sorry, you said you stayed there for how long? One month?"

"Yes. When I couldn't take it anymore, I packed my things and left. Didn't even tell Lee anything. I even let him keep the deposit. I just wanted out of there."

I'm honestly just glad to know that Helena isn't a psycho that wants to hurt me. Her story about the apartment is disconcerting, but I was frankly more worried about her, instead. I feel like there's nothing more to say.

"I should really get going." I get up.

Helena gets up, too. "Please, just listen to me. Find a new apartment."

The intense stare is gone, replaced by something akin to desperation.

"Look, even if I wanted to, I can't just pack my things and leave. I'd need to find a new place, and it would need to be affordable, and—"

"I'd be willing to let you stay with me until you find a new place. I have an extra room. Please, just leave that place."

Maybe Helena Myers isn't as normal as I thought she was. Either that, or she's extremely superstitious.

"Thank you for your time," I say with a smile.

I see myself out of the apartment and give Helena one final glance. She gives me one angry look before slamming the door shut in my face.

Although I'm feeling better after talking to her, there's a nibble of doubt that I can't get rid of. Something that makes me wonder if maybe she's right. Maybe the apartment really is haunted.

Chapter 19

On my way out of the elevator, I bump into Lee.

"We gotta stop meeting like this." He smiles.

There's no animosity to his tone. I could be wrong, but he seems completely fine with how we left things. No grudges, no anger. Not even awkwardness. At least not on my end, and he sure doesn't seem to be showing it.

"How's your day going?" I ask.

"Good. On my way to buy some meds for my mom."

"How is she?"

Lee's smile drops. "Not too great. She doesn't talk much these days. Sometimes she looks like she remembers me, but those are moments that go away way too quickly."

"I'm so sorry to hear that."

"It's okay. That's life." He shrugs. "But what about you? Everything okay on your end?"

"Yeah. I've just been feeling sort of tired lately. I have trouble waking up in the morning no matter how many hours I sleep."

"Hm. Make sure you get sleep at the proper time. Research says sleep is the most important between midnight and two a.m."

"I'll keep it in mind, thanks."

Lee nods and we're staring at each other for a moment. There's no sexual or romantic tension this time. The only thing that runs through my mind is whether I should tell him I spoke to Helena Myers.

"Well, I should go buy Mom's meds." He hooks a thumb toward the elevator.

I'm about to let him go, but something in me doesn't let me.

"Hey, Lee? One more thing," I say.

"What's up?" He holds the elevator doors open.

"I found another message in my mailbox. Like the one from before."

"Those damn kids again, probably."

"No, not exactly."

"Oh?"

"Yeah. You know, there was something that kept bothering me about it. So yesterday, I went back to security to check the footage."

Lee nods, but he looks uncomfortable. "Uh-huh."

I wait a moment before asking the next question. "It wasn't teenagers. It was a woman. Helena Myers. Your previous tenant."

I can see the color draining out of Lee's face. He looks like he's just seen a ghost.

"I know you weren't honest with me, Lee" I try not to sound accusatory when I say that. I genuinely just want him to know I know.

"What do you know about her?" he asks.

It sounds to me like he wants to gauge what I know so he can decide whether to lie to me or not.

"I spoke to her just now. She's the one who left those messages to me."

Lee scratches the top of his head and steps out of the elevator. The door closes and the elevator ascends to the ninth floor.

"I was afraid this would happen. What did she tell you?" he asks.

"Something about the apartment being haunted."

Lee squeezes his eyes shut and shakes his head. He raises a finger to his temple. "Andrea, look. Yes, I lied to you. I'm sorry about that. But the reason why I did it was because—"

"You wanted to protect me. You wanted to avoid me worrying about a crazy person. I understand," I interrupt him.

He looks surprised. "You figured it out, too?"

"That she's a little on the looney side? Yeah. Her stories were outlandish."

Lee breathes a sigh of relief. "I thought she would get into your head. You see, uh… we didn't part on great terms."

"Really?"

"Yeah. She's been troublesome since day one, always knocking on my door to demand I fix things she clearly broke on purpose, making lots of noise, and so on. I couldn't tell at first she was sick. Only after she moved in, but by then, it was already too late."

"So, what happened?"

Lee crosses his arms and looks down. "She came to me a little less than a month after moving in demanding her deposit back. Said she'll be moving out and needed the money. I told her it was short notice, but wanted to give her her money back anyway. The problem was, I didn't have enough, I had already spent a lot of it that month on my mom's medication. She became super angry, trashed my apartment, and threatened to ruin my life."

"Jesus."

"Anyway, I thought I saw her close to the building a few times, but I could never catch her before she ran. Not like I knew what to tell her, anyway. She wasn't doing anything bad as far as I knew. But then when you got that message, I knew it was her, and I lied to you about the pranking teenagers."

"You should have just told me the truth right away."

"Andrea, I want you to know that I never lied to you out of selfish or malicious reasons. I did it because I know you, and I know you'd worry. I didn't want you to be uncomfortable in your new home."

I smile, flattered by the gesture. "I understand. And thank you for being so thoughtful."

"I'm sorry things got out of hand so much."

"It's not your fault. Don't worry about it, okay? I know you can be trusted. Helena can't."

Lee looks relieved. "Thank you, Andrea. I'm glad you understand."

There's more silence between us, which is a clear indication there's nothing more to say, so I say, "I should probably let you get back to it."

"All right. I should get my mom her meds. She's probably impatient by now."

He calls the elevator, and once it arrives, he steps inside and says, "Andrea, if you see Helena nearby, don't hesitate to call the police, okay? We don't know if she's a danger to others, and I don't want her anywhere near you."

"You got it," I say.

The elevator closes. I waltz into my apartment, kick off my shoes, and I open the fridge. I'm hoping I still have some wine in there.

The doorbell rings again. Is that Lee? It has to be. Maybe there was something else he forgot to tell me. I wonder what could be so important that he needs to talk to me right away.

My brain tells me it has something to do with the kiss we shared. I keep trying to convince myself it's not that because Lee and I agreed nothing would happen between us. Despite that, I can't suppress the wave of unease that splashes me in the face.

I open the door and…

…it's Ryan.

Chapter 20

"Ryan?" I utter his name, blinking furiously in disbelief.

A myriad of questions runs through my head. How did he find me? What is he doing here?

I don't even have time to consider all the other questions before he speaks up.

"Hi, Andrea. Sorry to stop by like this. Can we talk?" he asks.

Oh, come on. You can't be serious. It's been months. I blocked him on two numbers. Can't he take a hint? Can't he just let me live my life?

"What are you doing here, Ryan?" I ask.

"You know why I'm here. I wanted to see you," he says.

"How the hell did you find me? Did Becca tell you where I live?"

"No, Becca had nothing to do with this. Come on, you know how persistent I am. It was only a matter of time before I found you." I open my mouth to protest, but he raises a hand to interrupt me. "I promise I won't hassle you. I just wanted to talk with you, that's all. Just one final conversation, and then you'll never see me again. Okay?"

It almost sounds convincing. I could spend the next ten minutes telling him to go away and still not have him listen, or I could get the conversation over with. I know Ryan, and I know he doesn't quit when he really wants something.

It's been two months, and him standing at my door tells me he's really hurting and really wants to see me. It's selfish. What about my pain? What about what I want? Has he even stopped to consider that he might be hurting me by constantly trying to contact me?

Two months.

Anyone else would have given up by now. I wish I could say I'm not swayed by his fight for me, but I am. He *really* cares about me, I suddenly realize. I don't think I was ever that important to anyone else except my parents. I'm so flattered that I almost forget why we broke up in the first place.

"Please, Andrea. I just want to talk to you," he says.

I know Ryan. He never wants to *just talk*. This "final" conversation won't be final. He's hoping for a Hail Mary. Something that will get me to change my mind and take him back. It's manipulative. It doesn't matter that his intentions are good. By coming here he's going to hurt me.

I can already imagine myself replaying the encounter with him for the rest of the night, remembering emotions I'm so desperately fighting to keep locked up.

Maybe I'm just dealing with too much right now, or maybe I miss him. Maybe I don't have the patience to deal with his stubbornness. I can't tell.

Either way, I let him inside.

"Thank you," he says as he enters the apartment.

The first minute is filled with awkward silence. A lot of unsaid things stand between us. It's how it always is for people with a history. You're staring at a person you knew like the back of your hand, but now they're a stranger to you. Years of intimacy gone, just like that, but the history of them remains.

That's what always makes it so awkward. Talking with a stranger is less daunting than talking with a stranger who knows everything about you.

"Nice place you got here," he says, and I can see a flicker of familiarity in his eyes.

It's painful because it momentarily gives me a sense of normalcy, a peek into the past where everything is okay.

Worse than that is the instinctive need to share your day with the person you're no longer familiar with. So many times, I had the urge to call Ryan to tell him about the things that happened in my life. So many times, I automatically thought about how I couldn't wait to get home to see him, only for reality to kick in.

"I know you're not here to talk about the apartment, Ryan," I say.

I'm determined to stay visibly indifferent in front of him. It's probably not working. He knows me as well as I know him, and he can probably read me just based on the tone of my voice, my body language, the speed at which I speak.

I suddenly feel too exposed in front of him, but I do my best to hide it.

Ryan nods. He takes a seat on the couch. I sit next to him but maintain my distance. It's not that I don't trust him as much as I don't trust myself. If I get too close, I might end up doing something I'm going to regret.

I just want to get this conversation over with so he can leave and I can continue living my life.

Seeing him on the couch of my new place makes me realize what a mistake I've made by letting him in. For a brief moment, I can almost imagine the two of us living here. I'm already remembering with more potency the history we've shared, and I know I'll probably spend the night tossing and turning, thinking about things a lot more clearly.

"How have you been?" he asks.

"Fine," I lie. "You?"

"Not great."

It's a bait. He wants me to ask why so he can tell me he misses me.

"Hope things get better for you," I say insincerely.

"I missed you," he says.

A little abrupt, but the sentence works wonders for me. I feel warmth slithering up my limbs and toward my torso.

Get a grip, I tell myself.

I don't tell him *I missed you too* even though I want to. Becca would be so disappointed in me if she saw me now. What do I even tell her? How do I tell her I let Ryan inside?

"I know. You don't want me being honest like that," Ryan says. "But I had to tell you. I think about you every day."

"You need to let me go, Ryan. We tried to make things work, and we couldn't do it. You're torturing not only yourself but also me. Did you even stop to consider my emotions in all of this? Do you think the breakup was easy for me?"

"I honestly can't tell sometimes," Ryan says with a somber tone.

"Well, it wasn't. It still isn't. You think you're the only one going through a tough time? You're not, because I miss you, too. But that doesn't mean I'm going to run into your arms just because I'm vulnerable. Breakups are hard, Ryan. We both knew this was a possibility when we started dating."

"I know," Ryan says.

I see the corner of his lip curving ever so gently into a smile. He's heard the *I miss you too* part, and that's all he needs. He already thinks he's won me back.

"Andrea," he says as he scoots slightly closer to me. "We can work things out. I promise. We'll make drastic changes."

I groan because I really don't want to listen to him trying to win me over. Again.

"Ryan… We've been through this a million times. You know things won't change."

I'm already working toward it. I started applying to new jobs so I can ditch the dead-end job I have now."

"Really?"

"Yes. And I changed other things in my life, too. You were right, Andrea. I was too cocooned in my comfort zone. I'm changing that now."

"Ryan, you know you can't change things just because you think I want you to. That's not how things work."

"I'll admit, you were the one who made me rethink my life, but I'm not doing it for you. I'm doing it for me."

I don't say anything because I'm not sure I believe him. This all sounds too convincing, but it also sounds like a desperate man's attempt to get me back. Who's to say things won't go back to how they were before? I can't go through a breakup again. I can't get my hopes raised.

I just can't.

"Look," he says. "I've had two months to think about this. I thought things would become easier after a while. They didn't. Every day, I come home from work and all I can think is, you should be here, but you're not. I don't see my life without you in it, Andrea."

His hand gently lands on my thigh. I don't swat it away, even though I know I should.

He's leaning closer to me.

What am I doing? Why am I not stopping him?

I can't make excuses for myself anymore. I'm not tipsy today, and I can't blame my decision-making on stress or whatever else. No, this is all me. Just like it was when I kissed Lee. I did it because I desperately needed the comfort of another man.

But that's not the case right now. This isn't a need for comfort. It's a need for Ryan.

I want to kiss him, and I'm too weak to resist the urge.

Our lips brush gently at first, and then we're making out. It feels like I kissed him just yesterday, and yet, it's like years have passed at the same time. I fully give in to his kisses and touches. My whole body is electrified.

At the back of my mind, I'm aware that Becca is going to be so immensely disappointed with me, but I don't care. I long for Ryan's touch, and nothing can dissuade me from getting it, I don't care how much of a loser I am for going back to him.

At one point, I'm lying on my back on the couch while he's on top of me and kissing me. I'm past the point of no return. I'm gonna go through with this with Ryan.

What happens after sex, though?

We might realize we're no longer compatible. No big deal. Ryan will get dressed and go home and we'll never talk again. At least we'll have a conclusion.

What am I saying? Of course it's going to be a big deal. Even if nothing happens after this, even if we never see each other again, this will all affect me. And I just started to get over Ryan. I don't think about him as often, and everything doesn't remind me of him, and I can listen to songs without crying like a baby all the time.

But we might go back to the way we were before. If we do, it could be a beautiful thing. It's going to be a hassle to tell all our friends and family, especially since we had made the breakup so public—I was the one who insisted on it exactly because I wanted to avoid falling into this trap.

The moment you say yes to him is the moment you'll allow yourself to be drawn back into that relationship again, Becca had told me.

What happens tomorrow is not my concern right now. I lead Ryan into the bedroom, and we begin taking our clothes off.

***

Lee is stifling a sob.

He's standing at Andrea's bedroom door, peeking toward the bed. Her ex-boyfriend—no, her boyfriend—is on top of her. He's watching him thrusting into her and listening to her moaning.

They're both so entranced that they don't see him. Not that they would, anyway. They turned off all the lights in the apartment.

Tears are trickling down Lee's face. He sniffles, but they don't hear him from the moaning and the squeaking of the bed.

Andrea's breaths are growing louder and more high-pitched with each thrust. She's reaching climax. That should have been him. It should have been him sleeping with her there, not this loser ex-boyfriend of hers.

Despite being heartbroken worse than he's ever been in his life, Lee's crotch is aching with a rock-hard bulge. He can't control himself. He takes his manhood out and begins stroking it. Ryan pulls Andrea up into a sitting position. Her head is thrown back and her eyes closed as she lets out shrill gasps.

If she only opened her eyes, she'd see Lee. Maybe not at first, but if she stared at the door long enough, she'd see something different about it, and she'd realize it was a head peeking at her.

The thought of it arouses him even more.

He has to put a hand over his mouth as he climaxes, shooting streaks of white on the floor in front of the door.

The post-orgasm clarity kicks in right away.

Peeking around the corner with his limp tool in his hand, careful not to be seen in his own apartment while the woman he loves is getting railed on the bed he bought, he feels like such a loser. He feels like everything his high school crush Tammy Harrison told him he was when she caught him peeping at her in the locker room.

Worthless. Sick. Pathetic. Creepy. Disgusting.

Many other names come to his mind, all raining down to shit on him while he's at his lowest. Tammy Harrison was right. That's exactly what he was back then and what he is right now. It's never him the girls pick. It's always the douchebag.

The realization of what an utter failure he is makes new tears blur his vision.

Andrea's moaning no longer arouses him. Each gasp she makes is like a dagger to his heart. The louder she moans, the greater his pain.

When he can no longer listen to it, he spins on the ball of his feet and storms out of the apartment through the secret passage. He closes the concealed door behind him just in time to hear both Ryan and Andrea let out shrill cries, which are then followed by deafening silence.

In the corridor, Lee collapses sideways into the dirt and dust, and he sobs like a little baby.

Chapter 21

"What was that?" I ask.

"What was what?" Ryan asks.

We're both out of breath from the intercourse, but I'm sure I've heard that sound just seconds ago—something that sounded like a slam.

"What did you hear?" Ryan asks.

"I don't know. It sounded like a door," I say.

"Hold on. I'll check it out."

He gives me another juicy kiss and puts his underwear on. He takes a step out of the living room and then his head snaps down.

"Ugh," he says.

"What is it?" I ask.

"There's something wet on the floor here."

Never mind about that right now. Just check the apartment, I think to myself.

Ryan steps into the living room, and after a resounding click, light bathes it.

I perk up my ears as I listen to his bare footsteps on the floor. The anticipation is killing me. When Ryan doesn't say anything, I call out to him.

"Ryan?"

There's no response. I wait a moment longer, and then I hear something shatter in the kitchen. Immediately, a lump forms in my throat.

Crap, crap, crap.

I was right to assume that someone had broken into the apartment. What am I supposed to do now?

On instinct, I get out of bed and follow Ryan into the living room. I'm careful about stepping around the splotch on the floor—where did it come from, anyway?—and I see Ryan standing in the middle of the living room.

"Ryan?" I call out.

He jerks his head in my direction then points at the floor. "Sorry, I broke a glass."

I huff. "Don't scare me like that."

"Why? Were you worried something happened to me?" He grins.

"Of course I was," I say.

He approaches me and pulls me to himself, "Don't worry about me, baby. I'm built like a tank."

He picks me up and takes me over to the sofa. He starts kissing my neck and caressing me. I reach my hand down to his crotch and feel that he's ready for the next round. He must have been really eager to see me.

I would much rather talk to him right now so we can figure out where we stand, but that's fine. There will be plenty of talking done later.

***

Lee listens as Andrea starts moaning again, from the living room this time. It's like she's come closer just so she can taunt him.

He's not going to stay and listen, though. He's afraid that, if he does, he might do something he will regret later.

The tears are still coming, but he wipes them away and suppresses his sobbing bout. As the sadness leaves his body, anger makes its appearance.

It should have been him there with Andrea. She rejected him and let her ex-boyfriend screw her. Is Lee really so lousy that some pathetic ex-boyfriend is better than him?

Yes. Yes, he is. At least Tammy Harrison would say so.

He can't get her face out of his head right now. That beautiful but arrogant face that made fun of him so much that he still sometimes thinks about her at night.

Lee remembers the first time he saw her in school, beautiful, surrounded by her mediocre friends. Her smile lit something up in Lee and he couldn't stop staring. He saw her almost every day in school, and it wasn't long before he started to undress her with his eyes.

She never knew about it. She knew who he was, and they'd even made brief eye contact once, but she was oblivious to his existence and his profound love for her. She was the first person he climaxed to. Back then, he didn't know how exactly masturbation worked. He just touched himself because it felt good, until one day, he accidentally came with Tammy in his mind.

From there, his horizons opened up.

He would come home from school and masturbate imagining them naked in bed. He would watch porn with actresses that resembled Tammy. He once even stole a picture of Tammy that he proceeded to masturbate to.

The more he obsessed over her, the more his desire became insatiable. He had to get closer to her to take a better look at her somehow. He just had to. He had almost gotten away with peeping at her.

She and her cheerleading classmates had just finished practice and were stripping in the locker room. Lee had hidden inside one of the unused lockers and was waiting for them to show up.

The girls were going to take a shower, so they stripped entirely. The sight of Tammy Harrison's naked body glistening with sweat awoke something inside Lee he hadn't known was there. Reality was so much better than the fiction in his mind.

Tammy's body was far from the perfection compared to the actresses in porn movies. Her tits were cup-shaped, the nipples protruding forward. She had a thin layer of fat on her stomach. Her ass jiggled with every step she took.

Those flaws were exactly what made her so perfect in Lee's mind. She was human, just like him, and yet, she was a goddess.

Lee put his hand inside his pants and rubbed his tool. By then, he'd already practiced enough to know what kind of a grip and stroke brought him the most pleasure.

The girls were standing in the locker room, chatting naked, unaware of his presence. The other girls were hot, too, but no one came close to Tammy. She embodied something more than just physical beauty. Lee had been close to climaxing when an audible moan escaped his mouth.

That was what caught the attention of the entire locker room. It didn't take long for them to locate the source of the sound. When they swung the door open, Lee was caught standing with his hand in his pants, a stain adorning his crotch.

The reaction of the girls was mixed—some gasped in shock; others laughed. A few of them snapped pictures of Lee in his embarrassing moment. Not a single one had a flattered reaction like in the porn videos.

One of them went to get a teacher. Lee tried running, but Tammy and the other girls blocked his path. He was cornered.

Tammy Harrison approached him. She bit her lip as she did so. "You like peeping, you dirty little creep?"

That humiliating remark awoke yet another kink in Lee he later fantasized about so often.

"I'll let you touch my boobs if you touch yourself right now," she said.

A few suppressed giggles came behind her. Lee still to this day doesn't know what he was thinking when he believed her. Perhaps it was the immense desire to touch her breasts that disabled him from thinking properly.

It was the same potent desire that he now has for Andrea; a painful, insatiable hunger that follows him day and night.

He took his thing out again, which was rock-hard, gripped it firmly, and stroked it. The curious and stifled mocking gazes of the girls turned him on. He barely had a few seconds to do it when the locker room burst into laughter.

"Can... can I touch them now? You said I could touch them if I do it," he said.

Tammy let out a peal of mocking laughter.

"Are you for real, dude?" she asked. "You think I'd ever let a creep like you get within ten feet of me? You're disgusting. You're a disgusting, sick, pathetic, and worthless creep."

More laughter.

That's when the student who went to get help returned with the P.E. teacher. Lee was sent to the principal's office, and his parents were called to the school. He got suspended for a few days, but things didn't stop there.

When he returned to school, the first group of students who greeted him was the jocks. One of them was Tammy Harrison's boyfriend. He had heard what happened, so he and his friends forced Lee into the bathroom where they beat him up and dunked his head in the toilet.

If that wasn't bad enough, the entire school knew about it, and he'd become known as Peepee Lee. There were days when he wouldn't be able to walk past the school hallway without hearing girls giggling or showing the small penis sign with their thumb and forefinger.

One night, he followed Tammy Harrison home. She wasn't aware of his presence. He didn't like her anymore. At least, not the way he used to.

He felt very angry with her, and the thought of hurting her aroused him. He fully intended on throwing her into an alley that night, ripping her clothes off, and having his way with her, but what stopped him was her boyfriend, who rolled out of nowhere in his Toyota and picked her up.

He noticed Lee and shouted a derogatory remark before driving off with screeching tires. Lee heard him and Tammy laughing as they took off.

It was a good thing he was stopped that night. Had he done something, he probably would have ended up in prison.

Eventually, he dropped out of high school.

He never became an architect like he told Andrea. That was a lie he told her to look more interesting to her. He did learn a lot about construction, though. That's how he managed to build an apartment that allows him to spy on Andrea.

But seeing Andrea wrapped around Ryan and producing those intimate sounds that were meant for Lee's ears, he feels the same hate and anger toward her as he did toward Tammy Harrison.

He let her into his apartment for dirt cheap. He helped her find a place of her own and escape from her toxic ex. He helped her carry in the boxes. He fixed things in the apartment for her. He's been nothing but nice to her.

And how does she repay him?

By rejecting him and going back to her ex-boyfriend.

That stupid, disgusting bitch.

Lee has had enough. Maybe he's been the nice guy long enough.

Maybe it's time to do something about it.

No, be patient. Be patient.

Acting rashly will only make sure his plan goes down in flames. No, he has to be smart about this. That's what Lee is.

Smart.

He may be disgusting, pathetic, sick, creepy, and worthless, but he's smart. He didn't need to graduate from high school or college for that.

He needs to get Ryan out of the picture, and then there will be no one to get in his and Andrea's way of happiness.

You're mine, Andrea. You just don't know it yet.

Chapter 22

Ryan stays over after we have sex. We don't talk about our relationship or what the future holds for us. Instead, we lie in bed naked and chat about random things. We laugh like we used to. The strangeness between us is no longer there. It all reminds me of the first time we had sex because it was exactly like this back then.

Maybe time away from each other was exactly what we needed in order to succeed as a couple. I feel more connected to Ryan again and like we're in the first stages of dating and in love with each other.

I'm optimistic. I really think we can make it work this time.

To someone looking at me from the sidelines, I might look foolish and crazy, but I don't care. I don't care if it makes me weak, either.

I *want* to go back to Ryan, and I'm going to do it. If things don't work out and I get hurt again, then it's going to be my own fault, and I'll gladly suffer in silence.

"So, what happens now?" Ryan asks after we're done talking about random things.

"I don't know. We go back to the way things were before the breakup, I guess?" I shrug.

"You really think we can do that? Go back to how things were before?"

"I don't see why not. It's going to take some effort from the both of us, but if we really want it, we can make it work."

He smiles at me. "I love you, Andrea."

"I love you, too."

Ryan stays the night. In the morning, he has to go. He asks if I want to move back in right away, but I tell him I can't do it just like that. I need a few days to get my things in order here, first. Secretly, I also want to take some time and see how I'm going to digest all of this, just in case.

Who knows? I might change my mind and think this was a bad idea. It's easy to come to a decision when euphoria is high.

In case I am sure, though, I'll have to go talk to Lee and thank him for his hospitality. I think I'm going to let him keep the deposit because he's already done a lot for me by letting me stay here so cheaply.

"You want me to help you take your things back to our place?" Ryan asks when he's at the door.

Our place. He hasn't said *my place*. It could mean nothing at all, but I see it as a sign that he's truthful about wanting a future with me.

"Sure. I'll take you up on that offer when I'm ready," I say.

He gives me a kiss and leaves. I already miss him. Absence makes the heart grow fonder, the saying goes. I can certainly see the truth in it.

For now, I have to go to work. When I return home, I'll talk to Lee.

***

Lee furiously paces the living room back and forth. His hands are clenching and unclenching. In a fit of anger, he flips the coffee table, causing all the trays and cups to crash onto the floor.

His mother is in the room, and she's staring at him in silence from that blasted wheelchair. She doesn't say anything, just watches him judgmentally as he throws a tantrum.

This is one of her moments of lucidity. It won't last long, but while it does, Lee feels like he's no longer in control. When she's herself, she's not afraid of him because she knows he can't hurt her, and that irks him.

Earlier, Lee snuck into Andrea's apartment while she was at work. He lay in her bed for a while and went through her clothes and sniffed them, enjoying the scent. He stole one pair of her panties from the drawer and brought them back with him.

No matter what he does, though, the black hole in his stomach refuses to shrink. She isn't his anymore, no matter how much he tells himself otherwise. And soon, she'll be gone forever, just like Tammy Harrison.

After Lee flips the coffee table over, he continues standing in the middle of the room, breathing heavily, staring at the mess. The TV is still broken, too, from his last fit of rage.

The entire living room looks like a grenade went off in it.

"Are you done?" his mother calmly asks, penetrating the silence.

He pivots in her direction. She still looks cool as a cucumber.

"Done throwing a tantrum like a little brat?" she asks. "Maybe now you can tell me what's been causing you to behave like this since last night."

"Andrea," he says through his teeth. "She made up with her ex-boyfriend."

"Good. I don't care how bad her boyfriend is; he can't be as bad for her as you would be."

Another wave of anger flares up in Lee's temples. He kneels in front of his mother's wheelchair and starts yelling in her face, "This is all your fault, you old bitch! If it weren't for you, Andrea and I would have been happy together! She would—"

A loud crack in the room silences Lee mid-sentence. It takes him a moment to understand his mother has just slapped him. He never understood how slaps managed to calm down panicking people in movies and TV shows. Now he does.

"You shut your dirty mouth, boy," Lee's mother says. "You're going to let that girl go, you hear me? And when she's out of here, you will never, and I mean *never*, look for her again, do you understand me?"

Lee wants to wrap his hands around the old woman's throat and strangle her. It would be so easy to snap her neck with just one squeeze. But he can't kill this woman. She's his mother after all, no matter how much he hates her.

His face contorts into a hateful grimace. "You stupid, old, demented—"

Just then, the doorbell rings, interrupting his insult.

His head snaps at the door, and he stares at it for a long moment. His mother lets out a shrill guffaw.

"Do you want to guess who that is?" she asks.

She continues laughing, and in that moment, Lee sees Tammy Harrison in that wheelchair, and not his mother.

"You need a time-out!" he says as he stands up.

"Go ahead. Lock me up," his mother says as he rolls her into the bedroom. "It won't change anything. When you open this door, you'll still be sick, and the girl still won't be yours."

The urge to strangle her morphs into an urge to kick her in the face with his heel.

The doorbell rings again. No time to deal with the old bitch now.

Lee slams the bedroom door in his mother's face and locks it. He walks over to the front door, composes himself, smiles, and opens it.

***

"Hey," Lee says.

"Hi," I say. "Sorry, I know it's getting late. Do you have a minute?"

I didn't mean to talk to him today, especially since I'm so sleepy after being awake most of the night and working all day, but I want to get it over with as soon as possible. It's going to be awkward, and I hate awkward conversations. I just want him to know how grateful I am for everything he's done, and I hope that one awkward kiss we shared stays unaddressed.

"Um, yeah. Sure," he says.

He steps outside and closes the door.

"Sorry, I'd let you in, but my mom made a mess in the living room. It's pretty gross, so it's best if we talk here."

"Oh, okay. No problem. Is she doing okay?" I ask.

"Yeah, don't worry about her." He dismissively waves a hand. "What did you want to talk about?"

"Well, um…" I scratch my cheek, unsure how to start and what to say exactly. "I wanted to inform you I won't be staying in the apartment any longer."

Lee's face drops like an anchor. I've never seen a smile disappear from someone's expression so quickly. It's as if I've just told him his entire family got killed.

"Oh," he says.

He's trying to look unfazed, but I can tell how much it's impacting him. I want to believe that the only reason the disappointment is there is because he needs to find a new tenant. That's why I'll offer to leave the deposit to him.

"Is something wrong with the apartment?" he asks. "Is it because of what Helena has told you? Because you know you can't believe what she says, right?"

"No, nothing's wrong with the apartment, Lee. And no, Helena has nothing to do with my decision."

Lee nods.

I say, "Listen, that deposit I gave you? You can keep it. You've been nothing but kind to me, and I want to return the favor somehow. I hope the money helps with your mom until you find a new tenant."

He nods absent-mindedly, but my proposal doesn't seem to make him feel any better.

"Okay, um… Can I ask why you're moving out?" he asks.

Now he's making it way too personal. I feel like I'm drawn into an emotional argument that I wasn't supposed to be a part of in the first place.

What do I tell him? I don't think he and I are close enough for me to talk about my private things, but I also think we're more than just a landlord and tenant.

"Is it because of me?" he asks before I can give him a proper response. "Did I do something to make you want to leave? Because that wasn't my intention. I care about you a lot, Andrea."

Okay, this is getting way too serious for my taste. Why is he telling me he cares about me? And why does it sound like I'm so important to him?

"No, no. It's nothing like that," I say. "You did nothing wrong. Things just happened in my life."

"Is it Ryan?" he asks.

I'm taken aback by his question. He must realize this, because he says, "I heard a man's voice at your door this morning. I figured it was him."

That's a little creepy.

"I'm sorry," I say. "I'd like to not talk about my reasons for moving out. I just wanted to thank you and to let you know ahead of time in case you wanted to look for another tenant."

I'm not a confrontational person, and I'll usually do everything in my power to avoid a conflict, so I surprise myself when I say what I say to Lee.

He nods. "I see. When do you expect to be out?"

"I'm not sure. Maybe even as soon as tomorrow, I guess?"

I don't know how it's possible, but Lee's face droops even more. It's in that moment that I realize just how much he likes me. It's not just like. It feels like way more. He's not taking the news I broke to him lightly at all.

I was thinking that, in the worst-case scenario, Lee would tell me how sorry he is that I'm leaving and wish me luck.

This, though? It's almost scary.

"Thanks for letting me know," he says.

He's taking it with dignity, at least, even though he looks like he's about to start crying.

"Sure," I say. "Thanks for being so hospitable while I was here, and for helping me fix things when I needed it."

"Yeah."

He looks like a zombie.

"Well, I'll let you get back to your thing," I tell him and turn around to leave.

"You're making a mistake, you know," he says when I'm halfway down the hallway.

I can't tell if it's just a statement or a warning. It sounds like it can be both.

Slowly, I turn around to see Lee staring at me.

"With your ex-boyfriend, I mean," he says. "He's going to break your heart again. If you want, I can keep the place vacant for when you want to come back."

What do I even say to that? I'm so freaked out all of a sudden that my brain refuses to form a single sentence.

I don't know if it's instinct or something else, but I turn around and rush inside the apartment.

"Andrea, wait!" I hear Lee calling out, but I ignore him.

Once I'm in, I deadbolt and lock the door. I'm hyperventilating.

Something about that encounter freaked me out so much, and I can't even tell why.

My gut instinct tells me I should leave the apartment tonight. I should call Ryan and tell him to pick me up.

No, pull yourself together, I tell myself.

There's no need to panic. What am I even panicking about? There's no reason for it, and yet, I can't calm down. I decide I could go for a shower to get rid of the anxiety attack.

***

Lee steps back into his apartment. He can tell he scared Andrea. That wasn't his intention. He wanted to let her know that he's a good guy and he's willing to help her.

Why is it that whenever he tries to do something good for the people he loves, he ends up scaring them off? Why do they always refuse to see his kindness?

He leans his head on the wall, resisting the urge to whack it over and over until his skull splits open. He wants to scream.

His mother's cough comes from the bedroom, and he only then remembers that he still needs to deal with her. He's had enough. He will no longer take her crap. It's time to be rid of that parasite once and for all.

Doesn't matter she's the woman who gave birth to him. She's a bitch and a whore, just like all women are.

Lee unlocks the bedroom and opens it. His mother's head is raised at the ceiling, scanning it as if there's something interesting up there.

"Hello, Mother," he says.

His mother looks down at him but then focuses on the ceiling again. She's in one of her episodes again. Shame. He wanted her to be aware of what he's going to do to her. He wanted to see the fear in her eyes as life drains out of her. It doesn't matter.

"Let's get you to bed, Mother," he says.

He picks her up easily since she barely weighs anything and gently lays her on the bed. She continues looking at the ceiling, muttering something under her breath.

He could inject her with her meds and cause her to overdose. It would be that easy to kill her. But she doesn't deserve an easy death. No, not his mother. Not the woman who was supposed to love and support him but tripped him at every turn instead. There's a special place in hell for bad mothers like her, and Lee personally hopes she burns there for all eternity.

He climbs on top of her and wraps his hands around her neck. She still doesn't acknowledge him. Only when he squeezes hard does she start fighting with an intensity he hasn't seen in her in years.

It's futile, though. She's old and frail, and he's young and strong. She has a remarkable will to survive, though, and it takes Lee almost five minutes to snuff the life out of her. By then, his forehead is covered in sweat and his fingers hurt from the tension.

When his mother finally stops struggling, he folds her hands over her chest, gives her a peck on the forehead, and slides into the secret passageway to pay Andrea a visit.

Chapter 23

I feel groggy in the morning again. I woke up in time for work, though, so that's good, but I feel as though five coffees wouldn't be enough to properly wake me up.

The first thing that greets me on my cellphone in the morning is a message from Ryan.

Hey babe. Sleep well?

A message from him brings a smile to my face. I really love this entire *we're dating from scratch* thing again. I know it won't last forever, but I'm okay with that. I'm enjoying the moment.

Before heading out of the bedroom, my eyes fall on the night camera facing my bed. Oh, that's right. I left it on last night. I press the button to stop recording and take a mental note to check out later whether I've been sleepwalking.

A part of me hopes this will all go away the moment I move back in with Ryan, that it's all just stress from being away from him. Maybe I should have told him to stay the night. He would have been able to tell me if I did anything strange in my sleep—if we got any sleep, that is. Whatever it is, I'm sure things will go back to normal when I return to Ryan's place—our place.

I really missed that bed. I know I said my neck hurt from it, but I don't think it's the bed as much as it's the fact that Ryan is going to share it with me. Things are going to be different this time. I just know it.

I type out a message to him. *I just remembered that I have to go to the doctor after work. Can you pick up my things sometime today and take them home? I'll leave the key to the apartment under the doormat.*

Does that mean you've made your mind up? he asks.

173

I send him a smiling winking emoji.

Everything is already packed. I finished doing so last night, and now the place looks like it did on the first night when I arrived. It feels so strange to be moving out so soon, just when I was starting to get used to the place, but I'm not complaining. I'm heading to something better.

I hope.

Sure, no problem. I'll pick your things up, Ryan replies to my message.

On my way to work, I call Becca. I have to tell her the news, not because I'm excited and want to share it with her but because I'm dreading her reaction. I assume she's not going to be thrilled.

My assumption turns out to be correct.

"What?!" she screams into the phone. "Andrea, please tell me you're joking."

"I'm sorry, Becca. I know I've failed you," I say.

"Girl, this is exactly what I was telling you about! The moment you say yes to him…"

"I know," I interrupt. "Look, I'm perfectly aware of the risks. And I'm aware you must think I'm a loser."

"I'd never think of you as a loser. I just feel like you're still vulnerable and you don't know what you're doing."

"I've had two months to think about this, Becca. I'm going to move back in with Ryan."

"Look, you're my friend, and I'm going to support you, no matter what you do. But because you're my friend, I have to warn you that you might be getting into something that'll end with you hurt again. And I doubt you'll be able to find an apartment as good as that one."

"I know. And I appreciate you supporting me, Becca."

"I can't believe you chose Ryan over your landlord, ugh," she says.

That prompts me to remember my last conversation with Lee. I suddenly can't get his hurt face out of my head. My lips are inadvertently pulled back into a rictus as a cringe.

As much as I'd love to continue chatting with Becca and tell her about Lee and everything else, I've arrived at work and have to go. I tell her I'll call her soon and head inside.

***

Lee is lying in Andrea's bed. He's gently running his hand up and down the pillow where she sleeps, imagining her lying next to him, staring at him, whispering softly to him.

How he misses her.

He can still smell her on the sheets, but that redolence is tainted by the stale sweat of another man.

He lies there, staring at the ceiling, imagining the future he and Andrea could have had together. He can no longer cry. His eyes are completely dry of tears. Now there's only anger and bitterness. After a while, he grows tired and falls asleep.

He wakes up sometime later. He doesn't know how long has passed.

Lee stands up and walks around the apartment. He stares at the couch where he and Andrea kissed. He sits in the same spot, imagining that night. He pictures Andrea sitting in front of him and leans in to kiss her. Warmth envelops his body and face as he inches closer to her.

He closes his eyes and...

Thin air is all that comes in contact with him. He stiffens his lips and lets out a frustrated growl. He stands and walks into the bedroom. Just as he's done so many times, he pulls out the drawer where she keeps her panties and sniffs them.

They've been washed, but there's a hint of Andrea's smell on them, just enough to get his imagination going. He gently puts the panties in his mouth and sucks on them. It usually does something for him, but not now.

There's only pain now, so he returns the panties in the drawer and slams it shut. He walks into the bathroom. He remembers watching Andrea taking a bath. He remembers them touching themselves together. It was such an intimate moment, and Lee longs to experience it again.

He sits on the edge of the tub and runs his fingers along the rim.

"I love you so much, Andrea," he says, his voice cracking.

Just then, the lock on the front door clicks. Lee hears the front door opening and then a deep voice. "Yes. Okay, I'll be sure to let them know. Thank you."

It's Andrea's boyfriend.

Chapter 24

"Hi, I have an appointment today," I say to the nurse at the desk when I arrive at the doctor's office.

She's young, in her early twenties, maybe. Her nametag says Tammy. She's the one who was working here last time, too. When she looks up at me, she smiles and asks, "Andrea, correct?"

"That's right," I say.

"I'm sorry to inform you your doctor has an emergency today, and he won't be able to see you," Tammy says. She looks uncomfortable when she says it, and I wonder if she often has situations where patients yell at her for something that isn't her fault.

"What? No one has told me about that." I'm surprised.

"The doctor had to leave just fifteen minutes ago."

"And I assume he won't be back any time soon?"

"We don't know. We're really sorry."

"It's okay. It's not your fault."

"Would you like to reschedule the appointment to another date?"

"Sure. Whenever the doctor's available."

"One moment."

Tammy turns to the computer monitor. She types something on the keyboard briefly before facing me again.

"The doctor can see you next Monday afternoon. Would that work for you?" she asks.

"Sure. Is there anything available at six?"

"Yes. I'll put you down for then."

"Great. Thank you. But listen, I was supposed to get some blood test results today. I don't suppose there's a chance I could get them before my next appointment?"

I don't even care if I need a doctor to read them for me, I just want to see what deficiencies I have in my blood so I can Google them and see how screwed I am.

"Oh, sure. Give me one moment please," Tammy says.

She gets up, disappears in the backroom, and comes back minutes later with a folder adorned with the clinic's logo. "Here you go. Your results. And I've put a reminder of your next appointment inside."

"Thank you so much, Tammy. You have a great day."

As soon as I'm out of the clinic, I read the results. There are a lot of things I don't understand here, but luckily, the results also show the normal ranges, so I can tell that most of the things are okay.

Most of them.

Except for one.

The result showing that I've tested positive for benzodiazepines.

***

Lee peeks out from the bathroom. He can see Ryan standing in the middle of the living room, looking left and right. He's scanning the boxes on the counter left by Andrea.

He picks one up and walks toward the door, but then he stops.

"What the…" he says when his eyes fall on the blank wall.

Except it's not blank anymore. Lee has left it cracked open so that the secret passage is visible.

Ryan places the box on the floor and prudently approaches the wall. That's when he steps out of the bathroom and starts sneaking up to Ryan.

His hand is firmly gripping the hammer he's brought with him.

***

I'm so confused.

What does this mean? How did these drugs get into my system?

I don't take meds. Is it possible that I've ingested some food that might have elevated what shows up in the test results? No, that's ridiculous. Certain foods can raise certain things in the blood, but only by a little. What my results show for benzodiazepines is way above the threshold, which can only mean one thing.

Someone has been drugging me.

***

Ryan peeks into the secret passage. Lee can't see his face from here, but he imagines a look of stupid confusion.

Lee has stopped a few feet behind him, the hammer dangling from his hand. He can't suppress the smile on his face.

When he grows impatient enough, he clears his throat. Ryan jerks around, his eyes wide.

"Who the hell are you?" he asks.

He tries to sound tough, but Lee can recognize the fear in his voice. Ryan is somewhat athletic, but Lee is stronger. And he has a hammer.

"Stay away from Andrea," Lee says as he steps toward him.

Ryan's eyes fall on the hammer in Lee's hand. By then, it's already too late. Lee has already swung the tool at Ryan's head.

***

I call Ryan, but he's not picking up. He might be driving or busy with work. He has the kind of job where he can get called at any moment to drive to the office.

I figure I should head directly back to his place since he's off work by now, but I then remember that I haven't packed some things. I'll have to go back to the apartment and pick them up. So, that's what I do. I sit in my car and drive back, my mind racing while I try to decipher the mystery of the drugs in my blood.

Who could have done that to me? Someone at work? It had to be someone at work. I don't go out anywhere much, and I certainly don't go out to the same places all the time. Even if I did, I don't see the point in a barista drugging my Starbucks coffee.

There's something unspooling inside me, like a dropped toilet paper rolling uncontrollably on the floor. With each minute that passes, my panic and paranoia grow. I need to talk to Ryan as soon as possible. I have to tell him what's going on.

By the time I arrive in front of the building, I've already tried calling Ryan four times. I left a voice message for him, so I hope he responds soon. I'm starting to become worried, though.

With so many crazy thoughts running through my head, it isn't long before I consider the possibility that it's Ryan who's been drugging me. That can't be the case, though. I've been feeling tired like this after we broke up, and I still feel like this even when we're together.

It's a ridiculous, momentary thought that I dismiss immediately.

I climb up to the fourth floor—using the stairs, of course, because Samantha from floor nine has occupied it with her baby stroller—and reach down to get the key from under the doormat.

Except, when I look under, it's not there. A jolt of panic goes through me at the thought that someone else might have found the key. I look up and realize the door is cracked open.

At this point, my heart is hammering against my chest.

I push the door open but remain rooted to the floor. My living room comes into view. Nothing seems out of order.

Nothing except one of the boxes sitting on the floor in front of the blank wall.

"Ryan?" I call out.

No response. The apartment is deafeningly quiet.

Someone was definitely in here, but was it Ryan?

My eyes gravitate to the floor, and I only just then notice the tiny red droplets there. Something messed up is going on. The panic is now squeezing my chest like a vise. With shaking fingers, I try to call Ryan again, but it leads straight to voicemail.

I feel like crying. What's going on? Am I overthinking things, or is something bad really happening? It seems like too many things at once to be a coincidence.

Okay. Calm down. I'm sure it's nothing. This can all be explained.

I go into the bathroom to make sure no one's there then into the bedroom. I open the drawers to retrieve the jewelry I forgot to pack earlier. Just as I stand, my eyes fall on the camera, and I remember again that I recorded myself sleeping last night.

I pick up the camera and sit on the bed, entering the recorded footage. The camera has a really neat option to adjust the speed to various levels so that I don't need to spend eight hours reviewing the footage, kind of like the security footage in the building.

For the first two hours, nothing happens. I watch myself in the green hue of night vision as I sleep peacefully, occasionally changing positions.

Then, something obscures the camera at around 2 a.m. I first think it's a glitch or something, but then the veil shifts, and I can see myself in the room again, but I'm no longer alone.

Standing next to my bed and next to me, while I'm sound asleep, is Lee.

I let out an audible gasp as I pause the video. I can't be seeing this right, can I? This cannot be possible. It's gotta be a mash-up of videos glitching out. It's gotta be.

I rewind to the moment when Lee first visibly enters the frame and play the video at normal speed.

He saunters over to the side of the bed and watches me sleeping. He's kneeling in front of me for minutes, just watching me in silence. I shift a few times but remain unaware of his presence. I watch as he reaches into his chest pocket and pulls something out.

I can't see at first what it is because the picture is too pixelated. But then I see him removing the blanket off my leg and I realize what it is.

A syringe.

My hands are trembling so violently that I can hardly hold the camera. My entire body is shivering as if I have a fever. My throat is closing up, and I can't draw proper breath.

In the video, Lee returns the syringe to his front pocket, stands, and pulls the blanket off me. I continue sleeping. I'm screaming at Andrea in the video to wake up, please, just wake up and fight back, but of course, it doesn't happen.

I don't remember any of this because he's been drugging me.

The next part makes bile climb into my throat. It threatens to shoot out of my mouth before I gulp it back down. Do I really want to watch what happens next?

I can already tell what's coming, and I'm still holding on to the hope that it won't happen, that none of this is real. I keep hoping for that even as Lee takes off his clothes... and mine.

The entire time, I remain knocked out and in my head, the words of Lee's mother ring out in my head over and over like a gong at close proximity.

Get out get out get out get out!

I'm whimpering. I don't even realize it until a tear falls from my eye onto the camera screen. I can't stomach watching this anymore, but I can't bring myself to stop, either. I have to know how far Lee has gone. I have to know how much he has violated me. I have to—

A knock sounds on the front door.

"Hello? Anybody home?" a voice asks.

It's Lee.

Chapter 25

I can't let him find me like this.

Oh God, what do I do?

"Hello?" Lee calls out again.

His footsteps enter the apartment. If he sees me with the camera, I'll be in so much trouble. He doesn't know about the camera, that much I'm sure of. If he did, he would have deleted the footage, just like he probably did in the security office when we went there together the first time.

I have no choice. I put the camera back into its spot where it remains nicely hidden, wipe my tears, sniffle, and walk out into the living room to greet Lee.

When he sees me, he smiles. "Oh, hi! Sorry for barging in like this. The door was open, and I wanted to see if everything was okay. I hope you don't mind."

I brush my hair behind my ear. "Yeah. I was just getting ready to leave. Ryan will be here with Becca and Jacob to pick me up soon and help me move out."

I want Lee to know someone knows I'm here and he'll be in trouble if he does something.

"I see. Well, I won't take up your time, then," he says.

"Thanks."

The entire time, there's a visibly huge distance between us, one that I hope doesn't betray my fear. I can't make myself get any closer to him. Just the sight of him disgusts me beyond words. But more than that, I'm also terrified. I feel like I'm standing in front of a whirlpool that will suck me in and drown me if I take just one step closer.

Lee walks up to me and asks, "Since you're leaving, how about we share one glass of wine as a farewell?"

"I should really get going. I need to be ready for when Ryan comes," I say.

"Oh, come on. Just a quick drink. Five minutes tops. I'll help you with those boxes if you need it. Just like first time. Remember?" He smiles, but I can't help but think there's a threatening message behind those words.

I'm afraid he might step closer to me, and he's already close enough as it is. Instead, he turns around, walks into the kitchen, and grabs a wine bottle from the fridge.

"I have to say, you were the best tenant a landlord could ask for," he says as he pours wine into the glasses.

He's in an awfully good mood. It contrasts how he was yesterday so much that it feels like talking to another person entirely.

As if there's something he's not telling me.

"Come on, Andrea," he says as he raises his glass and leans against the counter.

If I give him what he wants, he might leave me alone. No, that's wishful thinking.

He's not going to let me leave just like that. Still, I need to buy myself time while I think of a way out of here.

My eyes drift to the front door. If I'm fast enough, I can be out of here before he catches me. No, too risky.

I'll play along for now and get out of here when I grab the chance to do so.

I walk up to the counter and take the glass he's poured for me.

"Here's to your future," he says. "May you get treated exactly how you deserve."

Our glasses clink. I bring mine to my mouth, but I don't sip. Not in case he's put something in the wine.

"I hope you enjoy your new life, Andrea. Humans are strange, don't you think? When things go bad, we wish they were better. But when we already have a great life, we still wish we could have it better. We don't see the bad stuff because it's so far behind us. We're ungrateful like that."

"Yeah." I force a smile.

"You okay? If I didn't know any better, I'd say you're not too happy to leave," he says.

"Just waiting for my boyfriend to come pick me up," I say.

"I see." He takes a sip. "Is he really coming, though?"

"Yes," I retort almost instantly and realize it's a mistake. "Why do you ask?"

"Are you sure he hasn't changed his mind? Exes tend to do that."

My gut twists into a knot. What has he done to Ryan?

"I'm sure. I spoke to him just a few minutes ago. He'll be here soon."

Lee nods. He takes another sip of wine, places the glass down, stares at it for a moment, then says, "You're a terrible liar, Andrea."

I know in that moment my cover is blown. Lee is no longer trying to conceal his malicious intentions. He doesn't need to because he doesn't plan on letting me out of here alive.

"I'm sorry, what?" I ask.

"Ryan came by here earlier," Lee says.

My heart rate is going crazy.

"What did you do to him?" I ask.

"Everything I did… I did it so you would understand that you don't need anyone but me. I can make you happier than Ryan or anyone else in this world, Andrea. I can protect you. I can give you everything you want."

He's making his way around the counter and toward me. I recoil and backpedal.

"I love you, Andrea," he says.

My eyes fall on the object in his hand.

A syringe.

He's planning to drug me again. My survival instincts kick in. I've never been in a fight in my entire life, but when Lee approaches me, something starts controlling me. Just when he reaches me and is about to jab the needle into my arm, I swing my hand at his face.

The glass of wine smashes over his forehead. There's a loud shattering sound. Lee groans. His eyes are immediately closed from the broken glass that rains down on his face. I take that opportunity to run past him. The door is right in front of me. All I have to do is run out into the hallway and—

My hands are yanking the knob, but it's not working. The door is firmly stuck. It takes my discombobulated and panicked mind a moment to understand the door is locked, not stuck.

I spin around to see Lee still standing in the kitchen, blinking furiously. Shards of glass are stuck in his face. Our eyes meet, his shoulders tense up, and I know I'm out of time.

I run toward the bathroom because it's the closest door. Lee's hand grabs the hem of my shirt, but I manage to pull free. I run inside the bathroom and lock it just in time for Lee to slam against it with his entire weight.

"Andrea!" he shouts and bangs on the door.

That persists for barely a few seconds before it stops. Silence envelops the apartment.

Something's wrong. I can feel it. Something is coming. He wouldn't just leave me alone like this. Not after that.

I run to the sink and open the cabinets below it. I rummage through the cluttered junk in search of something I can use as a weapon. Various things clatter to the floor and I go through useless makeup and pill bottles.

Scissors.

Too small to inflict serious injury but good enough to stagger Lee if I can hit him at the right angle. I straighten my back and adjust the grip on my newfound weapon so that it doesn't slip from my hand.

My eyes fall on my reflection in the mirror, which looks ghastly. A layer of sweat covers my forehead, my hair is messy, and my eyes are wide like saucers.

A loud shatter explodes right in front of me and I recoil and scream.

When I look in the mirror again, it's no longer my reflection but Lee, and he's climbing into the bathroom.

Chapter 26

Andrea is terrified of Lee. He can see it on her face. It isn't the reaction she was supposed to have. Not with him.

He doesn't even care anymore. He tried being good to her. He tried to show her how much he loves her, and she refused to accept it.

Now, she's going to pay. He's going to kill her, just like he wanted to kill Tammy Harrison because that's all she deserves. That's all sluts like them deserve.

***

I can hardly believe what I'm seeing. Lee climbing in through the mirror.

At first, my frazzled mind thinks this is some kind of an otherworldly experience, but then I see the dark room behind the shattered mirror. He's been watching me this entire time. If there weren't for the adrenaline pumping through my bloodstream, I probably would have puked from the sickness that grips my gut.

Lee looks furious. The veil of compassion that he's had on his face this entire time is gone, replaced by his true expression: An unfiltered hatred directed right at me.

Once my moment of confusion is over, my brain screams at me to run for my life.

I spin around and fumble with the bathroom door lock. I hear glass crunching under Lee's feet as he steps inside the bathroom.

The lock clicks, and I swing the door open. I run back out into the living room, panting and whimpering. What the hell do I do? What should I do?

Lee is coming closer. He's taking his time, and I wonder if he's trying to allow fear to brew in me. I would have run toward the front door had my eyes not fallen on the blank wall in the apartment.

Except it's not blank anymore.

Of course it isn't. How have I never seen this before? I feel so immensely stupid as I stare at the secret passage yawning at me. That's how Lee snuck inside. He used the secret passageways to get in. I feel so goddamn stupid for not noticing all the red flags earlier. And with that, comes unbridled anger.

There's no time to contemplate all those things, though.

Lee is closing in, and I won't have enough time to unlock and open the front door, so I do the only thing I can—I run into the passageway.

"Stop!" Lee shouts at me.

I hear his stampeding footsteps as he breaks into a dash toward me. I slink into the passageway. I'm instantly blinded by the darkness, but I feel the walls around me and run in the only direction the passage forces me. I hope to God I won't run into a dead end. If I do, it's game over for me.

No. I still have the scissors. Those are my Hail Mary in case Lee catches up to me.

Cobwebs tickle my forehead, but I hardly register them as I run. I'm not even aware of the cut on my hand. There's a slight burning sensation, but it's nothing in the face of the fear that inflates me.

"Stop, you bitch!" Lee shouts after me.

He's getting closer. I try not to scream as I quicken my pace. The passage is straightforward, but I can hardly see anything in the darkness, even as my eyes adjust. I blindly stumble forward as fast as I can, but Lee sounds like a speeding truck behind me.

I suddenly see a pale source of light to my right. Hope surges through me when I see it. I don't waste time thinking where the gap might lead. I slip inside.

Only then do I turn around to orient myself. I'm in a bedroom. There's a wardrobe out of place in front of the hole I just sidled through.

Without thinking, I push the wardrobe that's out of place against the wall, though I doubt it will do anything to slow down Lee. I spin around and scream when I see a face staring at me from the bed.

It's Lee's mother. Her eyes are glassily staring at me, unblinking, unmoving. Her mouth hangs open.

She's dead.

I let out another scream just as something loudly crashes into the wardrobe behind me. I instinctively take two steps back and cover my head with my hands. There's a deafening thud and crack as the wardrobe topples mere inches from me. It would have crushed me had I not stepped back just in time to dodge it. Lee is staring at the entrance. He's no longer holding a syringe in his hand but a hammer stained with blood.

Oh, Jesus Christ. Whose blood is that? Whose blood is it?

I run out into the living room, slam the door behind me, and lock it. Lee's banging on it follows immediately. I turn around to run, and that's when I see him.

"Ryan!" I shout as I fall to my knees in front of Ryan's body splayed on the floor. "Ryan, we have to run! Come on!"

I shake him violently as the door behind me splinters.

"Ryan!" I scream, but Ryan doesn't respond.

Maybe if I slap him, he'll come to. I turn his head toward me and notice the blood coating his temple.

Oh no.

I'm too late. He's already dead.

The door behind me breaks open. Lee lets out a guttural growl as he bursts inside.

I've wasted too much time, but the door is right there.

I clamber up to my feet and dash to the exit. My chest is already inflated to let out a scream for help.

Lee is much faster, though. Long before I reach the door, His hand grips me by the arm firmly, and he pulls me onto the floor.

"No!" I scream, my eyes plastered to the door.

It's so close. So close. If I could only…

Lee climbs on top of me. He's holding me by the neck with one hand. He's raising the hammer with the other, ready to smash my head in just like Ryan's.

I think it's all over for me, but then I remember the scissors in my hand. I don't know whether it's going to slow him down, but it's my only shot.

I grip the scissors so firmly that it feels like I'm going to crush them in my fingers. Then, I thrust them as hard as I can into Lee's arm. I feel the tips of the tool juicily digging into his flesh.

Lee Lets out a scream. His hammer hand falters. He reaches to take the scissors out, and that moment of hesitation is all I need. I pull the scissors out and aim for his neck.

The scissors pierce his jugular. He doesn't scream this time. He lets out a raspy breath as he claws at his neck. I push with all my strength. Lee falls off of me with ease.

He's on the floor, the scissors are out of his neck, and he's holding his hand over the wound spurting blood. My eyes fall on the hammer on the floor.

The door is right there. I can now leave. But I don't.

There's only one way out of this. And I'll be damned if I risk the possibility of this fucker surviving.

I grip the hammer and approach Lee. He sees what I plan on doing, and he raises his hand. His eyes grow wide in terror, and I revel in it. I raise the hammer as high as I can, and then I bring it down on him.

The first hit whacks his fingers, and I hear a loud crack coming from them. He lets out a yowl as his hand retracts. His forefinger and middle finger are twisted at unnatural angles.

While he screams in pain, his head is left open for an attack.

The second hit with the hammer silences him.

After the tenth hit, the squelching and cracking has stopped. All I can hear is the dull whacking of the hammer against the bloodied floor where Lee's head used to be, and myself sobbing. I only then realize Lee is no longer moving and his head is a mangled mess of blood, bone fragments, and brain tissue. The wood flooring has gone from light brown to dark red.

I drop the hammer and scoot away from Lee. I hug my knees and cry like a baby. With the adrenaline and the danger gone, it's okay to do that.

I don't know how long passes before I hear a voice.

"Andrea..." it mutters.

I immediately raise the hammer again, ready to strike Lee, but then I realize the voice is actually Ryan's. He's blinking in my direction, a hand over his bloodied head.

"Ryan!" I scream as I drop the hammer and crawl over to him.

I take his face into my hands. Our eyes meet, and he groans.

"Feels like the worst hangover ever," he says.

I hug him tightly and continue sobbing. He gently strokes my back for a long time.

"Help me up," he says.

I lift him into a sitting position, and he lets out another groan. His eyes fall on Lee's dead body.

"What happened?" he asks.

I shake my head. "I'll tell you everything later. For now, let's just get to a hospital."

Chapter 27

Ryan is exhausted. I can see it on his face when he walks into the apartment.

I smile and greet him.

"I missed you," he says as he leans to kiss me and plops onto the couch next to me.

I'd like to think that seeing me disperses his exhaustion at least a little. It's like that for me, at least.

"Me too. I've made us dinner," I say as I stand. "It'll be ready in three minutes."

"You're the best, babe," he says. "But you shouldn't be working when you're sick."

"I'm actually feeling better today," I say as I put food onto the plates.

"Are you sure? You seemed really sick this morning."

"I'm fine. Besides, sitting doesn't help me in any way."

"All right."

Ryan sits at the table, admiring the chicken and rice I've cooked. I've poured a glass of wine for him, but not myself.

I sit on the opposite side, pull my chair in, and pick up the fork and knife. Our eyes meet, and I force a smile. Truth be told, I'm still feeling sick, but it's mental more than physical. I'm hoping he doesn't notice something's off.

"You okay?" he asks. "You look a little down."

I haven't been the same since the incident at the apartment. No one can blame me for that. It would have been a terrifying experience for anybody. To know that your landlord has been watching you for months while you're sleeping, sneaking in, sexually assaulting you... and then to be forced to kill him...

Sometimes, I wake up at night when I hear something. I immediately prop myself up on my hands into a sitting position and I see Lee standing at the foot of the bed. I blink and Lee is replaced by an inanimate object I mistakenly thought was him.

I jump at the smallest noise when the apartment is too quiet and I'm alone. I check every nook and cranny to make sure no one's hiding inside. I look in the mirror and wonder sometimes if there's a person standing on the other side, watching me and doing perverse things.

No matter how many times Ryan checks if all the windows and doors are locked, I don't feel safe inside these walls.

And sometimes—I'm ashamed to admit—but I relive the moment I kill Lee. I close my eyes and picture myself stabbing him with the scissors and smashing the hammer over his head again and again.

It's never enough.

No matter how hard I swing the hammer, and no matter how deep I stab him with the scissors, it's never enough to lessen my hate for him and for what he's done to me. I wish it lasted longer. I wish I hadn't been so filled with panic so that I could watch Lee suffer before he dies.

Even if I killed him a thousand times, it would not be enough. He's gone, but in a sense, he's still with me. Doesn't that mean he's won in a way?

It's a miracle I'm still normal after everything that's happened, but then again, the dust hasn't settled yet. I might suffer from the fallout in the days to come. It's only been about four weeks since the incident.

"The thing with Lee is bothering you, isn't it?" Ryan asks.

I nod slowly.

Ryan reaches across the table and grabs me by the hand. He tells me the same thing he tells me every time I feel this way.

"Hey, you're alive. That's all that matters. Things could have been a lot worse. Lee could have entered your apartment at night. He could have raped you in your sleep. You're lucky he only watched you."

I feel like vomiting again. The smell of food is making me sick. I pull my hand free and force another smile.

Ryan doesn't know what Lee had been doing to me. I didn't have the stomach to tell him. Hell, if there was a magic pill that could help me forget I ever saw that video of Lee assaulting me, I'd gladly take it.

Ignorance truly is bliss.

Right now, something else is on my mind. I had morning sickness today, and I'm late. While Ryan was at work, I went to the pharmacy to get a pregnancy test. Those few minutes of waiting for the test to work were the most nerve-wracking of my life.

And then I saw those two lines that confirmed I'm pregnant. The most horrifying two lines I've ever seen in my life. For over an hour, I sat on the toilet, staring at it, refusing to believe I'm pregnant.

That's not how I imagined finding out I was pregnant for the first time. I was supposed to be ecstatic, jumping to the ceiling with happiness.

None of this makes sense. Well, it does, I just refuse to believe it because of what happened.

I refuse to believe it because I ran the numbers in my head, and no matter how many times I counted, the results are the same.

It's been almost four weeks since I left the apartment. Ryan and I had sex twice on the same night when we made up, but we used protection. But we weren't very careful that night. It's not impossible that he's...

If it's not Ryan, then that leaves only one possible conclusion, and I refuse to even entertain that thought because it's the stuff of nightmares.

Even now as I think that, I feel as though there's a parasite living inside me, growing, waiting to burst out of my womb and kill me. Lee's final fuck you to me. His attempt to make me his even when he's no longer here.

So yes, Lee is still with me, and not just in a metaphorical sense.

"Actually, there's something I need to tell you," I tell Ryan as I play with my food.

"You know you can tell me anything, babe," Ryan says.

I take a deep breath. How do I even tell him this?

If I tell him I'm pregnant, he's going to be very happy. Ryan has always talked about the possibility of me and him having a child. But then I'm going to have to destroy his hopes by telling him the full truth that I've kept hidden from him all this time.

What will he want to do? What do *I* want to do?

"What is it, babe?" he asks.

If I tell Ryan what really happened, it's going to change everything between us. It might even destroy us, and this time it's going to destroy us in a way that we'll never be able to recover.

"I'm pregnant," I say before I can give myself time to become too scared.

No going back now.

Ryan straightens his back. He stares at me with his jaw hanging open. He looks down at his plate then back up at me. He looks how I feel.

"I see," he says. "Um..."

He probably knows he should say something else to that, but he looks confused as hell.

"Are you sure? I mean..."

"Yes. I took a test this morning."

"I see. Wow."

He's staring down at his plate again. There's no happiness that I was sure would be here.

"Ryan? Are you okay?" I ask.

"Yeah. Yeah, I'm fine, I just... This blindsided me is all."

"I know this is a shock for you."

"It's not that, just... I don't know if I'm ready for kids. This is... I don't know."

"Really?" I ask. "I thought you wanted to have kids."

"Yeah. I did. I still do. It's just... I guess I wanted us to devote time to each other first, then get married, and then... This is too fast, I guess."

I'm the one who reaches across the table this time. I feel like I could cry tears of joy. "I'm so glad you feel the same way."

He looks like a weight has dropped off his chest like it's dropped off mine. "Really?"

I nod. Tears are blurring my vision. "Yeah. I don't want this."

I don't want this monster inside me, I really want to say.

He squeezes my hand back. "Hey, if neither of us is ready, then the answer is pretty obvious. We'll go to the doctor together, okay? I'll take a day off from work tomorrow."

I nod. I'm so relieved to have his support in this that I can't stop crying.

"Are you sure about this?" I ask.

Ryan smiles. "Yes, Andrea. I'm sure. I love you, and I want to make things work between us."

"Okay." I sniffle.

For a moment, I contemplate whether I should tell him the truth. I then wonder what good it will do. It will only divide us, and there's no need for that. There are some crosses we have to bear alone, even when we have the full trust of our partners, because we want to protect them from our darkness.

I smile as I squeeze Ryan's hand. "We have more than enough time in front of us. Who knows what the future will bring."

THE END

More Books by the Author

You'll never want to date again.

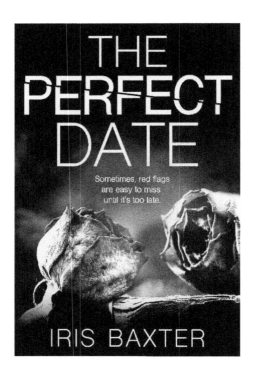

Available on Amazon

Printed in Great Britain
by Amazon

59759130R00118